MANUAL FOR HOW TO LIVE MAGNIFICENTLY

MANUAL FOR HOW TO LIVE MAGNIFICENTLY

stories

ERNIE WANG

ACRE
CINCINNATI 2026

Acre Books is made possible by the support of the Robert and Adele Schiff Foundation and the Department of English at the University of Cincinnati.

Printed in the United States of America

Designed by Barbara Neely Bourgoyne
Cover photograph iStock/Charles Taylor

ISBN-13 (pbk): 978-1-968209-10-0
ISBN-13 (ebook):): 978-1-968209-11-7

The press is based at the University of Cincinnati, Department of English, Arts and Sciences Hall, Room 248, PO Box 210069, Cincinnati, OH, 45221-0069.
www.acre-books.com

Acre Books titles may be purchased at a discount for educational use. For information please email business@acre-books.com.

CONTENTS

I.

LOSE MAGNIFICENTLY

FORTUNE OF FORGETFULNESS

They've rented the back room at Applebee's for Mature Singles Meetup. By the second hour, I've memorized their names, which are emblazoned on large tags pinned to print dresses and blazer lapels. Standing next to the platters of appetizers, Herb and Gladys snack on chicken wonton tacos and ask each other invasive questions. *Are you amenable to bad sex? What's your outstanding mortgage balance? Are you ticklish*? At sixty-seven and fifty-nine, they have neither the time nor the patience for pointless drivel.

Immaculately dressed Mabel Rogerson looks to have given up on meeting anybody tonight. She has instead directed her attention to drinking. Having abandoned wine spritzers for straight scotch, she stands in the corner, alone, and bops her head to the Bee Gees playing softly from the ceiling speakers. She leans forward, as if to join the slew of conversations that surround her, and in this moment, she looks alone and sad, like she might never meet anyone ever again.

I adjust my felt hat and stride toward her. My robe swishes, which reminds me I look ridiculous, but I have someone's night to brighten. Her eyes widen as she sees me approach. I whip out my crystal ball and thrust it toward her, just then remembering it's a snow globe. I couldn't find my crystal ball, misplaced somewhere in the depths of my bedroom closet.

"Would you like your fortune told, ma'am?"

She stares at me suspiciously, as though yet to decide whether to accept me as the fortune teller that I am tonight, and for which the organizers are paying me thirteen dollars an hour plus tips, or to dismiss me as a pickup artist.

"Tell me who you are," she says. "What is your name?"

This is a good question. One should always know with whom they are speaking.

"It's Mark Dekker."

"If you know my future, Mark, then you should know my name. What is my name?"

"Mabel Rogerson."

She covers her mouth with her hand. "And how old am I?"

She has forgotten the name tags have their ages as well, to expedite the matchmaking process.

"Seventy-one."

She gasps. "Very well," she says. "I would like to have my fortune told."

I nod sagely, as if I had known all along it would come to this. I raise the snow globe and shake it briskly. The flakes gently swirl around the fir trees and chimneyed cottage. I pause, then I shake it again, creating a second flurry. I narrow my eyes, the room darkens, and the others fade into obscurity.

"Mabel," I say, deepening my voice.

"Yes?" she whispers.

My voice rises to a shriek. "Maaaabel."

"Oh my," she cries. "Yes, Mark!"

I lower the globe. The snow settles. The room returns to normal. The chatter resumes. I hear someone say, "On a scale of one to ten, how would you rate your ability to control your bladder?"

"Dear Mabel," I say. "You shall indeed find what you came here for tonight."

Her mouth purses into an *O*. "I will meet a hunky man?"

"It is destined. And he will be very . . . hunky."

She smiles excitedly, then gives me the once-over. "As hunky as *you*?" she asks.

"Well I didn't say that."

"Oh." Disappointment flits across her face, but she quickly rebounds.

"He will emerge when you least expect it," I warn her. "So, you must be prepared."

She looks around the room. "What should I do until then?" she asks. She pats her hair.

"Believe in yourself. Remember how wonderful you are."

Her smile widens, and she leans forward to embrace me. I wrap her in my arms, the snow globe still clutched in my hand. After a few moments, I pull back, but she tightens her grip, so I dive right back in. When she lets go, her eyes are red and wet.

"Mabel?"

"I think I got what I came here for," she says.

I look at the ground. My shoelaces have come undone.

"What on earth would I do with a hunky man anyway?" she continues. "Make him lie down for a nap with me?"

She takes a sip of her scotch and sets the glass on the table. She is leaving, and I may never see her again. She grabs my hands.

"Mark." The scotch is sharp on her breath.

"Mabel."

Her eyes are tired and bleary and sad. "Are you aware your crystal ball is a snow globe?"

I'm still getting the hang of this divination thing. I moved back home to Dayton several months ago after Mom started calling me Chester—my absent father who Mom doesn't despise but I do—on our nightly phone calls. She's only forty-one, I had yelled at her doctor over the phone, to which he said, "I'm happy to answer any questions you might have, Mark," right before I hung up. The days with the most important person in my life were numbered, and I wasn't going to waste them anywhere but by her side.

Chicago wasn't really working out anyway. I had moved there hoping to become a weather forecaster, the job I'd wanted since I was a kid, but it turned out you needed college for that. All I left behind was a retail job at the mall.

She was lucid when I pulled into the driveway. "My dear Mark," she said, crying, and I wondered how much longer she'd get my name right. "It's OK," she reassured me, and I just stood there in her embrace, while she still knew it was me.

On the good days, Mom asks about Chicago, if I'd been to the top of the Willis Tower, if I could see all the way to Dayton. "I've always wanted to see the world from that high," she says wistfully. I ask her what I was like as a kid, trying to extract what memories she can recall before they lock up. I ask for stories of us. She tells me how I hated going to state fairs because the animals and crowds scared me, but I'd go anyway because I knew how much she enjoyed them, that her favorite part was getting funnel cake at the end of the night, and how that was my favorite part, too, because it meant we were going home, and for a moment I marvel at how brave I once was, and then from nowhere she says, "You look more like Chester every day, Mark."

The other days, which are becoming more frequent, are unbearable. She asks what it will take for me to move back, and I say, "Mom," and she snaps and says, "Don't call me that, Chester. Mark and I are hanging on by a thread." I sit there with my eyes shut.

"You're right, honey," I say, my voice cracking. "I'll do better."

"You make me so happy, Chester," she says, voice softening. She frowns. "Why are you upset?"

In the midst of this, I needed a job. Dayton isn't exactly the economic powerhouse that Chicago is, and even if it were, I'd end up serving ribs and strawberry margaritas anyway. So I answered the job ad for fortune tellers. If I couldn't forecast rain and storm, perhaps I could predict huge net worths and auspicious wedding dates. I went in for the interview, and they offered me the job on the spot. "You just have the look," they said, and when I asked, "What look is that," they shrugged and said, "Oh you know, it's je ne sais quoi," and that really impressed me.

They trained me in the art of divination for a week. It was mostly learning to pick up on visual cues. The high school kid looks insecure? Show him a future in which he is thriving and beloved. Lonely? Future lovers and friends will clamor for his attention.

So far, I've done three birthday parties, a farmer's market, a bar mitzvah, a quinceañera, and the most perplexing of them all: an AA meeting. I'm not sure what they expected, but I was sure of what I would not say. In their future, there was not a single drunk driving accident, not one case of cirrhosis. *I* do *see gainful employment in your near future. Your adult children* will *one day speak with you again.* Some thanked me, relieved. Others cried. I felt, for the first time, the weight of the authority I wielded with my crystal ball.

I have never felt as fraudulent as I did that night.

Sometimes at night, I lie in bed and try to glimpse into my own future. How long will I continue to tell people what they want to hear? When will Mom stop calling me anything at all? Who does one turn to when there's no one left?

I sink my face into the pillow. I wish I knew the answers to these things.

Mom insists on date night—"Mark always goes out," she says, "and so should we"—and so we drive to Columbus, where we spend the day at the state fair. We ride the Crazy Mouse coaster three times. She giggles on the initial ascent and through the sharp turns. Each ride drives me deeper into motion sickness and despair. Midway through the last run, I observe her just before the drop. She shrieks, then leans in and hugs me, and for a moment I feel the world is all right, I'm all right. Then the coaster drops, and I grit my teeth and curse as she squeals into my ear.

We make our way to the game booths, to the water squirt gun race, where I summon all my focus. I want to win her the grand prize: an enormous Elmo that dwarfs the other prizes lined in neat rows in the back. But the nine-year-old kid next to me drills his target with the precision of a sniper, then accepts the Elmo and smirks at me like a snot-nose. Mom hugs me and says the little plush tyrannosaurus was what she wanted all along, which mollifies me, but I stick out my foot when the kid walks by, sending him and Elmo hurtling to the ground.

No, I don't do that. "Congrats, kid," is what I say. "Enjoy your Elmo."

It's late now, and we're in line for funnel cake. The night is warm and sticky, and the fairgrounds are brightly lit with fluorescence and floodlights and green-and-orange glowsticks. Before us, a mother cradles her sleeping toddler on her shoulder. The toddler stirs, and the mother rocks him back to sleep. Mom observes them closely.

"Chester." Mom pats the tyrannosaurus. "I don't remember if we have kids." She shakes her head and laughs.

"That's funny!" I say. And because I can't help myself, "What would you name him if it's a boy?"

"Mark."

I'll take it. "If it's a girl?"

"Helvetica."

I pause. "I think that's a font."

"It's pretty," she says.

I don't disagree. We've made it to the front of the line. Emily, who's taking orders, smiles at us. The fair lights flicker in her eyes like fire-flies.

"We can't leave without funnel cake," I say.

Emily laughs and says, "You'd better not." Our gazes lock, and for a moment, I'm back at the top of the Crazy Mouse coaster track, inches from the sky, looking down at the people milling below.

Mom nudges me. "Chester," she whispers. I stiffen with frustration.

"One with strawberries, one with caramel," I mumble.

"You remembered my favorite," Mom says, sounding pleased.

This is what you remember? I don't say, handing Emily the money, wondering how it would be to go through life as Helvetica and, since I'm wallowing in self-pity, convincing myself I'd take that over Chester.

Emily hands us the funnel cakes in grease-stained paper bags. I scramble to think of something witty to say, but she has turned her attention to the couple behind us. Mom offers her arm. I stifle a sigh, and we head for the exit.

The road to Dayton is deserted. Our headlights cast two narrow beams into the night. The occasional truck roars by, then it is quiet again. The car smells like funnel cake.

"I had a wonderful time," Mom says.

"So did I."

"You mean everything to me," she says. She leans back and closes her eyes.

"Who means everything to you?" I whisper.

But her breathing has slowed. She has fallen asleep, her hands cradling the little tyrannosaurus.

"I can't do this for much longer, Mom," I say.

Her mouth curls into a peaceful smile. She tilts her head and snores softly.

"Just kidding," I say. "You stick around, and I'll keep being whoever you want me to be."

I focus on the road, and I feel more alone than ever as the headlights light up sign after green sign saying Dayton fifty miles, Dayton forty miles, Dayton next three exits.

There's nothing I dread more than corporate parties, where free alcohol mixes with exhaustion and months of pent-up office rage. An accounting firm has rented out Skateworld for their annual social event, which wasn't their smartest move. It hasn't been an hour and I've witnessed four people knocked to the ground. It's a white-collar roller derby.

They've placed me next to the snack bar. So far nobody's asked for their fortune. Instead, they ask if I went to college for this, where they can get a robe like mine for their kid's wizarding party, would I take a photo with them. *No I didn't, Party City, go right ahead.* A man stage-whispers to his daughter: "This is why you stay in school, sweetie." I thrust my snow globe toward the girl and solemnly nod, as if to say: *Listen to your daddy.*

Two drunk accountants who barely look old enough to drink shuffle by and gawk at me.

"Gandalf, is that you?" one says.

"You shall not pass," the other says, laughing at his own joke before letting out an audible fart.

"You shall not pass gas," the first says, and they howl.

I finger-pistol at them. "You," I exclaim, as their howling intensifies.

A man in his forties approaches from behind and cups their shoulders. They jump.

"How about you clowns put your skates on and go do some laps," the man says.

"Yes, sir," they say, glaring at me and slinking away.

I give the man a small wave. "Thanks."

"No problem." He squints. "*Are* you Gandalf?"

"I'm a fortune teller," I say. After a pause, "A fortune teller entertainer." After another pause, "I'm pretty much just an entertainer."

He asks what kinds of things I predict.

"How many kids you'll have," I say. "Which superhero you most resemble."

He smirks. "Tell me what my bonus will be this year."

"Twelve million dollars."

This pleases him.

"Tell me when I'll retire," he says.

"Three years, likely sooner."

He stops smiling. "Tell me when my daughter will speak to me again."

"What?"

"I've tried everything."

"How old is she?"

"Thirteen." He pauses. "I can't figure it out. She acts like I don't exist."

I want badly to tell him that I understand.

"Is that a snow globe?" he asks.

I look down. I've retrieved it from my pocket, and I'm mindlessly shaking it.

"I can, in fact, see into your daughter's mind."

"Oh?"

"I can see," I say, choosing my words carefully, "that she loves you very much. But she's in a difficult period of her life. She's having trouble expressing anything at all."

"What do I do?"

"Remember that she loves you, even if she doesn't tell you so." I swallow hard.

"You're shaking your globe again."

Indeed I am. I give it one final shake, then thrust it into his hand.

"Here. Have it."

"Huh?"

"It's no Magic 8 Ball, but it's gotten me through some rough spots. Maybe it'll help you until your daughter starts talking again."

He gives it a shake.

"It's peaceful," he says.

We watch the last of the snowflakes settle. I wonder if years from now he will begin to forget, if his daughter will look back on this period and regret shutting her father out. Now, he wishes he could tell her how much he loves her, if she would just let him. Years later, when it's too late, she'll wish the same thing.

"Well, nice talking to you," he says.

"Oh. Right. Nice talking to you, too."

"If you ever have kids, I wish you more luck than I have."

I shift my focus to the parade of glum accountants who silently circle the rink, the strobe lights casting a glittery pallor on their anxious faces, as though their thoughts are on the reams of paperwork that wait for them in the office, on the hours they could be billing if it weren't for this abhorrent party.

It's a bad day. I mean the worst day. Mom is feeling frisky. She's trying to pull me into her bedroom.

"Mark's asleep," she says. "He won't hear a thing."

I'm dressed for work, I'm exhausted, and I'm late to the birthday party.

"Chesterrr," Mom purrs. She looks at my costume. "What are you wearing?"

"I'm a fortune teller. And I need to get to work."

She smiles slyly. "I'll show *you* fortune." She reaches for me.

I swat her hand away.

She recoils. "Did I say something wrong?"

"No!" I steady myself. "No," I say.

"What's wrong, Chester? Is it me?"

I smile wanly. "No, babe. It's me. I really have to get to work."

She slips her arms around my waist. "Are you sure?" she says.

I pry myself free. My heart pounds. "Can you wait until after work?"

"I can't." She slides her hands over my hips. Her hands inch toward my crotch.

In my panic, I shove her harder than I should. She flies backward and gasps as she collapses onto the floor.

"Mom," I whisper. I am rooted in place as the room spins.

She cries softly and gazes at me. "I'm sorry that I upset you," she says.

I stare at her wincing in pain. I am, it turns out, just like my father.

I flee.

My job for this kid's birthday party is to follow orders. They don't want me ad-libbing. They've provided me with the script of the fortune I am to recite for the celebrant. They've also assigned me a special name. I am Fortuno. Fortuno the Fortune Teller. The script I've memorized is as shameful as the name they've assigned. *Your road to glory will be rocky but fulfilling. Patience is your ally.* It's as if they picked apart the pile of cookies at a Chinese restaurant and transcribed the entire script.

The party's in full swing by the time I arrive at the house.

"Look who's here!" the host calls out. "It's Fortuno! The Fortune Teller!"

I wave as if I'm on camera. In my mind, I see Mom collapsing onto the ground, over and over and over again.

They hand me a slice of cake, which I thank them for, then set aside, explaining that I need an empty stomach to perform at my finest. "Oh of course, Fortuno," they say in a hushed tone. I nearly vomit.

"Fortuno, can I touch your crystal ball?" a young girl asks. She grasps it with both hands and peers into it.

"What do you see?" I ask.

"My reflection."

I whisper into her ear, "That's the only thing a crystal ball can show you."

Her eyes narrow. "Your hat is stupid and you are a bad fortune teller," she says.

I snatch away the crystal ball. "You will become an insurance claims adjuster," I hiss, waving my hands wildly.

"I hate you, Fortuno," she wails, before bursting into tears and running off screaming for her mother.

"It's time! It's time!" the host chirps, gathering everybody into the living room.

I make my way to the edge of the crowd.

"We have a special treat today." The host beams. "We have Fortuno the *Fortune* Teller with us, and he will be foretelling a *special* fortune. Without further ado, I present to you . . . Fortuno."

To a smattering of applause, I reveal my crystal ball from under my robe. The crowd murmurs approvingly. They do not see my hands tremble.

I close my eyes. I see Mom on top of the Willis Tower, leaning toward the horizon. The wind blows, she squints in the sun. I wonder who she is smiling at. I wonder if it's me she sees in the crystal ball. I wonder if she knows who loves her back.

The room is quiet as they wait for me to begin. When I say nothing, they shuffle in their seats. A faint rustle simmers.

"Fortuno?" the host says.

I lower my crystal ball. "I'm sorry," I whisper.

The host stiffens, brows furrowed. Then he leans forward and smiles, as though he must have misheard.

"I beg your pardon, Fortuno?"

"My name is Mark," I explain. "I'm sorry. It's Mark."

MOTHER, MARKSMAN

Forty-six-year-old Yumi Kobayashi is not ashamed to say she's obsessed with League of Legends, an online video game in which the typical player is a maladjusted seventeen-year-old boy who smells like funk and nihilism.

Actually, this isn't true. Yumi is quite ashamed of her obsession, but she has no friends from whom to hide this secret. She is reclusive and alternately taciturn and prone to bursts of anger, similar to the behavior often displayed by the four randomly selected players she's teamed with, and occasionally she yells at her neighbors' plants, so she has alienated herself in this quiet town of Dayton, Ohio. And after a long day of serving passive-aggressive customers at Golden Peach, a Chinese restaurant where the bestselling item is chicken pad thai, and where her boss, Harmony Cho—a spoiled, nefarious twenty-four-year-old with the voice of an accordion—micromanages how she is to present the bill (humbly, with gratitude), all Yumi wants to do is come home and crack open a Sam Adams and annihilate her online opponents.

Actually, the biggest reason she spends so much time playing

League is to avoid expending energy worrying about her son, Chad, and what has become of him.

But she doesn't want to think about that now. She is exhausted from her shift and still annoyed over the table of customers who had told her, "You're so serious! You should be happy, like the Applebee's servers!"; she thanked them, her voice flat and dispassionate, and poured them more sweetened green tea, and she does not want to think about that, either, how she wishes they had been run over by a dump truck in the Golden Peach parking lot. She simply wants to focus on her game, in which she is in the late stages of a tense match. In the chat box, three teammates are directing their frustration toward the fifth player in the support role.

WARD our jungle you idiot

How are you this blind

You are literal trash

Yumi wishes they would stop picking on the support player and focus on the game, not because she feels sorry for him—she doesn't—but because she badly wants to win. But she keeps this to herself and instead funnels her attention to the screen, where she is playing Ezreal, the cheerful, chirpy, intrepid explorer, and boldly arcane-teleports behind enemy lines, catching everybody including her teammates by surprise and securing her team's victory. The familiar electric hit of euphoria floods her veins and her furiously pumping heart.

A message box pops on her screen before she queues for the next game. She recognizes the player name: *HellCat893,* her abused fifth teammate.

HellCat893: Great game! You're nice to support. Play again soon?

Yumi's hand hovers over the keyboard. She never chats during games. This is likely why *HellCat893* thinks she is nice: because she hadn't flamed him. Had she typed what she really thought, she would have told him to uninstall the game and stick to Minecraft.

Yumi thinks for a moment, then types: ok.

A response pops up: Where are you from? I'm from Oklahoma.

Yumi imagines a nineteen-year-old cowboy in chaps and midcalf boots, mouth stuffed with a gob of chew, hunched over his laptop and pecking away at the keyboard.

I'm from Los Angeles, Yumi types. Actually, she has never been west of Chicago, but she has always dreamed of seeing the Pacific from Mulholland Drive. She has no desire to reveal too much—anything, really—to an online stranger.

Whoa! *HellCat893* writes. Must be crazy partying there.

Yes, Yumi types. After a moment, she adds: Hell yes. Then: I party all the time.

She leans forward and reads the message on the screen:

How old are you?

Yumi panics and powers down her laptop for the night.

"We need to talk about your job performance," Harmony says after sitting Yumi down in her office during Yumi's break.

"Why?" Yumi asks. She serves cream cheese sushi rolls to clueless customers at a restaurant that claims to be authentically Chinese; isn't that performance in itself?

"It's part of the annual review process we do for all employees," Harmony explains. She opens her binder and traces her finger over the print. "Well, you're not doing *baad*," she says, emphasizing the *baad* so forcefully that it is as if Yumi were the worst server in all of Ohio. "But there is certainly room for improvement, wouldn't you agree?"

It's not that Yumi doesn't agree; it's that she couldn't care less about this job or her customers or if Harmony happened to slip and fall through a manhole and die a horrible septic death. But in the absence of any alternative employment, she sits quietly. She took this job assuming it would be temporary, after losing her position as a line supervisor at the local Honda office—they claimed insubordination, a claim she rejects—but she has been unable to find anything better since.

"Take, for instance," Harmony says, "your continued refusal to upsell our appetizers. Why won't you try to get our customers to order gyozas and satays?"

The reason, of course, has nothing to do with Golden Peach's appropriation of other Asian countries' cuisine. Yumi is too tired to get riled up about that. She just finds their appetizers so bland and overpriced that she would never be able to pull it off. *I recommend the crab rangoon!* She imagines herself gushing to her customers, then sticking her finger down her throat.

"The same goes for our desserts," Harmony continues. "You should always offer them the dessert menu, no matter how much of their main plates they leave unfinished."

Yumi concedes that their desserts—fried ice cream and banana sundaes and slices of cheesecake—are more palatable, and while she agrees she should try harder to sell these, typically by that point she just wants the customers to leave so she can collect her tip and not see them until the next time they come back for more of the same garbage. But she is sick of Harmony, so she promises she will try harder.

Harmony shuts her binder. "Good," she says. "That's what I want to hear. That you're striving to be a better employee and person. As your manager and mentor, that's all I can ask for."

Yumi imagines a world in which she has mastered karate, and in this world, she would slap Harmony so hard that Harmony would collapse into a state of disharmony for months—maybe years. This makes Yumi smile, which Harmony mistakes for acquiescence.

"Now get out there and show them what you've got!" Harmony exclaims, as if they are in a football locker room in the closing minutes of halftime, and Yumi springs from her seat and nearly shouts, "Argh, got it, coach!" but what Harmony does not hear, as Yumi exits the office and returns to her section, is the stream of expletives directed at Harmony coursing through Yumi's mind, so vile and shocking that even her pimply League teammates would have blushed had she typed them into the chat box.

* * *

Her shift complete, back in her apartment, Yumi brusquely knocks on Chad's bedroom door. She holds a ham sandwich. Her patience, questionable to begin with, has been reduced to a wisp. When Chad first broke down and withdrew from the world three months ago—a little after his twenty-fifth birthday—Yumi swapped her bedroom with his, in a rare moment of generosity, reasoning that he could use the privacy that comes with an en-suite bathroom. This turned out to be a catastrophic mistake; he hasn't emerged from the bedroom since. After two days, she began to leave food at his door, which he retrieved only after she'd gone to bed. Every morning, the sight of the empty dishes outside his door fills her with a seething annoyance that her duties serving food now extend to her home. Still, she drops off trash bags every Sunday and toiletries every other Wednesday, which he routinely, if invisibly, retrieves in the dead of the night.

Yumi knocks again. She wants to reassure him that she does not care for an extended, drawn-out conversation; she despises those in any case. A simple "last night's chicken teriyaki was good" would suffice. But she cannot bring herself to grovel just to hear his voice.

Yumi presses her ear to the door. Was that the creaking of his bed? Possibly. This, she admits, much like the flush of the toilet, gives her a sense of relief, this evidence that he is not yet dead, which in turn deepens her exasperation that it has come to this in the first place. There had been a period in Chad's life—lasting through third grade—when she could not get him to stop talking, despite her best efforts. Every waking moment was filled with his incessant musing and his pestering questions she had no idea how to answer: Mommy, do fox bite? Will Daddy ever come home? Why are your boobies so small? "Why do you care about any of these things?" Yumi had finally exploded, which sent him trudging to his room, snot-nosed and in tears. Then, every year thereafter, he gradually became quieter, which Yumi must have noticed with relief at some point, but she did not give it much thought, until one day he withdrew entirely, and then it was too late.

She places the sandwich by the door, calls out, "Food's here," and walks away, boiling. He should be handled delicately in his fragile state, she knows; still, she badly wants to tell him that his behavior is keeping her captive in the apartment as well, and that he should just get over himself.

She retreats to her room—previously Chad's room, still littered with his clothes and comic books—and powers up her laptop. The light of the screen glows green on her face in the dark room and reveals for the first time today her growing excitement and the hint of a smile. With the tinselly chime indicating her online arrival, two cans of Sprite and a small bag of Doritos at her side, at several minutes shy of eight o'clock at night, she has finally come alive.

Yumi is a marksman, the most difficult role due to a lack of mobility and the tendency to be instantly killed. And as the marksman is the most important player in the late stages, there is an expectation that her teammates—particularly the support player—will sacrifice themselves if that's what it takes to keep Yumi alive. Yumi understands the importance of the support role for her own success and does what she can to work seamlessly with them.

Except *SternErn*, who has been assigned support in this game, does not see it that way. Before the start of the game, *SternErn* asks her to swap, claiming that marksman is his main role, too. Yumi wishes she was better at support, but it is her weakest position, so she remains silent in the pregame lobby, as always, hoping he will relent. He doesn't. After she locks in Kog'maw, a lizard with the mobility of a sloth, *SternErn* locks in Vayne, a demon hunter with the durability of a fruit fly, and with that—their selection of the two marksmen most reliant on support—their team's fate is sealed.

Next time do as I say, *SternErn* types twenty bleak minutes later, as their team, down twenty-two kills, seven towers, and fourteen thousand gold, unanimously votes to surrender. For a moment, Yumi is tempted to respond with: *like your mom did when I told her to get down on her knees,* and she realizes that she is actually typing this out, so she closes the screen.

She exhales in anger and resists the urge to smash her keyboard—she does not want to work extra shifts at Golden Peach to pay for a new laptop. She reminds herself that as a middle-aged woman playing a game designed for adolescents, she needs to keep things in perspective, but the intensity and spectacle and thrill of the game nearly always throw her out of this mantra and reduce her vision to the singular, myopic lens of the petulant teenager.

She hears the arrival ping of a message.

Sorry about your terrible support.

It is from *HellCat893*, who must have been spectating her last game. Yumi considers whether to respond, then, after a moment, types: It's ok.

HellCat893 replies: And sorry about asking for your age the other day. That's not my business.

Yumi: It's ok.

HellCat893: Thanks. I'm not thinking straight these days.

Yumi: Everything ok?

HellCat893: Usual stuff. Boyfriend problems. Parent problems. I need to get out of OK asap.

Boyfriend?

Are you gay? Yumi types.

HellCat893: I'm a girl.

Yumi instantly feels empathy with her. League is a toxic game for everybody, but especially so for women, who often must endure misogyny and alienation to play.

Yumi types: My son is being an ass and won't come out of his bedroom and I need to get out of here too. Typing the words is a relief. She should do it more often, she thinks.

Hellcat893: Son? You're a dad?

"Shit." Yumi forgot that there is nothing about her that strangers need to know—how she can't stop tugging at her sagging skin at night, how her customers ask for ketchup for their bibimbap, how on her worst days, she is downright ashamed of being Chad's mother.

I meant my mom is being an ass. Lol, Yumi types, holding her breath.

HellCat893: Lol yeah I hate my mom too.

Yumi exhales. Then: Do you ever feel like locking yourself in your bedroom and never coming out?

HellCat893: I'd rather run away for good. Never come back.

Yumi: Me too.

She adds: Is there any reason why you might lock yourself in your bedroom though?

Lol, Yumi also adds. She tacks on a smile emoji, just to be sure.

HellCat893: I guess if I hated my parents so much that I was afraid I'd kill them then yeah I might not come out of my bedroom then.

Yumi quickly aborts mission and invites *HellCat893* to a game. For the next two hours they lose themselves in fierce clashes and epic dragon fights and tower defense and minion lane control, though Yumi cannot stop imagining Chad emerging from his room, eyes filled with rage, ready to do battle, as if she has been the enemy all along.

"A baby?" Harold said breathlessly, his eyes lit up with a brilliance Yumi had not seen in the three years she'd known him, first as her college chemistry lab partner, then—after they'd been drawn to each other by their shared love of adventure—as the oddball who whiled away rainy afternoons poring over maps and travel guides. "I'm going to be a father?"

Yumi sank into her chair. This was absolutely not the reaction she had been hoping for. What exactly that was, she wasn't sure, but this was not it—no, that wasn't true; she had hoped that he would bring up the idea of termination first. Her head hurt, and she felt bloated and nauseous.

"It's still early," she said. "Things can go wrong."

They were seniors at the University of Dayton and had recently moved into their first student apartment together. Though it was understood that they were embarking on the next steps, Yumi had assumed this meant less consequential things—they spoke frequently of traveling to New York and Tokyo and the Bahamas after graduation—

not her becoming a mother. Over the last four days, as she kept the results to herself, she had imagined how her new life would look and counted all the things she would no longer do and see, and, frankly, this made her want to vomit, as if she hadn't been vomiting copiously already.

"Should we find out if it's a boy or girl?" Harold asked, sounding giddy. "We can hold off, but if you want to find out soon, that'd be great, too. Oh Yumi, I couldn't ask for a better partner."

She smiled weakly. She told him she was tired and would be taking a nap.

"I don't know what to say," Harold said grimly two weeks later, his expression unreadable.

She simply wasn't ready, she had finally told him. They could try again when they were older, after college, after they traveled, maybe. What she kept to herself was that in those two weeks, she had realized her life was just beginning, she had a trillion countries to see, and she felt her sense of autonomy shrinking with each passing day.

It was either the three of them, or it was none at all, Harold coolly laid out three days later. His mind was set. He couldn't tell her what to do, but he would want to have nothing to do with her if she went through with the termination.

"Now I'm really going through with it," Yumi snapped, though inside she was reeling. His ultimatum had caught her completely off guard.

Harold changed tactics and begged her to reconsider, promising he'd bear the brunt of the responsibilities, as if that were even possible, which softened her a little, but not enough for her to change her mind. This was simply something that she could not adequately explain, and even if she could, she did not feel as though she had to.

On the morning of the procedure, he tried one last time.

"I want us to see the world together, Yumi," he said. His hands shook as he reached for her, and his words slurred from not having slept for a week. "Please. We can do this together."

In this moment, Yumi came as close as she ever would to truly loving him. When she drove off, she couldn't bear to look back to see whether he still stood in the doorway.

She had second thoughts the moment she entered the clinic. She didn't feel as though she were any different from the few women scattered in the waiting room—some with partners, some with mothers, others alone, like herself—and those she briefly spoke with were supportive and kind. But she was no longer certain. So, when her doctor, sensing her hesitation, asked if something was on her mind, she stood and blurted, "I'm going to have to discuss this with my partner," then fled.

On the drive home, she wrestled with how much to share with Harold. She still couldn't fathom any scenario in which she would risk her life for her child, and was that not a litmus test for whether one was ready to be a parent? On the other hand, the farther she drove from the clinic, the more certain she was that she didn't want to return. She was dreading confronting Harold, because she did not know what she would say.

When she entered the apartment, Harold was gone, along with his stuff. It was just her, and her swelling body, and her clinging to what remained of her future, a life already slipping away. She dropped out of college before she began to show—she never went back after coming home for fall break—and instead worked multiple jobs for as long as she could. And when she brought Chad—his cries as quiet as a kitten's—into the world, she basked in the tenderness she felt toward the strange miracle she held in her arms, but she had to concede that a part of her was still unsure whether she had made the right choice, a doubt she would carry for much of her life.

The young couple at Table Three are not enjoying themselves, and though the food probably isn't helping, the tension is coming from something else. From what Yumi has pieced together, they were supposed to be celebrating Young Woman's acceptance of a better job, but at the last second, apparently, Young Woman declined the offer, which she has revealed for the first time to Young Man tonight, and now Young Man is hysterical, presumably over the money that he will no longer enjoy being able to spend.

"I just don't want us to move to Chicago," Young Woman says as Yumi approaches their table and plonks down platters of Singapore noodles and Vietnamese pho.

"This was our ticket out of this dump," Young Man huffs, his voice low.

Noticing Yumi, they straighten their posture and force smiles and thank her.

"Oh, don't mind me." Yumi waves them off. Turning to leave, she mutters, "I would leave this shithole too, if I could," then catches Young Woman glowering like she wants to hurl the bowl of pho at Yumi's face.

When Yumi returns from the kitchen, Harmony is receiving an earful from Young Woman. Harmony remains silent, only speaking up at the end to apologize and to tell them that she will speak to their server. She comes straight for Yumi, grabs her elbow and hisses, "My office, now."

"I was just telling her the truth," Yumi says when Harmony demands an explanation, though Yumi recognizes her argument is tenuous. They both know Yumi knew what she was doing.

"Whose truth?" Harmony asks. "Why can't you just do your job and not make things so difficult? Now I have to comp them dessert, and there's no way they're leaving a tip."

Both of these things upset Yumi, because she needs the money, and she really wants the couple to leave. She should have kept her mouth shut.

"Look," Harmony says. "I know things aren't easy for you right now. But if you can please just do your job right, I won't have to worry about us going out of business."

"Fine."

The lines on Harmony's face soften. "How's Chad these days?"

That Harmony is aware of Yumi's personal life surprises her, and it is jarring to hear her son's name. "He still won't let me see him."

"I'm sorry. Does he speak to you, at least?"

"Also no."

Harmony sighs. "I'm sorry, Yumi. I have a three-year-old. I don't think I'd survive if he ever stopped talking to me."

This surprises Yumi as well, because Harmony has never given any indication that she, too, is a mother. Yumi assumed that somebody who was so enthusiastic about their food service job must have nothing better to focus on.

"Take whatever food you want from the kitchen tonight, OK?" Harmony says. "Save you one night of cooking, at least."

Yumi nods.

"And Yumi," Harmony says.

"Yes?"

Harmony points at Table Three. "Your customers still look pissed off. Go apologize again and give them dessert. Tell them it's on the house."

Seven months ago, Yumi tried to teach Chad to love League. Demonstrating a degree of patience that nearly broke her, she taught him the basics: to check brush for opponents, to look out for teammates, to equip his character with armor and magic resistance—essentially, how to survive. For two months, they sat side-by-side at the dining table for hours every night, laptop fans whirring from overexertion, Chad mostly silent, staring blankly at the wall or scrolling on his phone as she dispensed instruction and critique and game trivia with growing excitement. She marveled at how awful he was, confirming her suspicion that his helpless lack of coordination on the T-ball field years ago extended to his present-day mouse-clicking fingers, and she was irritated by his sitting posture—curled forward like a roly-poly. But she needed something to distract him from sliding deeper into the abyss, and she was running out of ideas.

They were alone in the enemy jungle, deep within lush foliage and thickets of nutmeg trees, a dark canopy looming above them. Their teammates were dead, and the three remaining enemies could have been hiding in any of the surrounding bushes, waiting to ambush them.

"What do you do?" Yumi—Caitlyn, the Sheriff of Piltover—asked. The butt of her rifle rested on her taut shoulder, and her open eye, wide and alert, pierced through the magnifier. She and Chad stood back-to-back. Chad, playing Taric—Pool Party Taric, at that—was equipped with a gigantic lifeguard megaphone. His hair was blond and flowing and fabulous.

"*What do you do*?" Yumi repeated.

Chad—Taric—dashed toward the closest bush, his vision ward in hand.

"No!" Yumi cried.

From the bush leapt Rengar, the lionlike predator, knocking Chad to the forest floor. Xin Zhao and Fizz quickly emerged, spear and trident raised high. Yumi watched helplessly as her son was punctured to death.

"Oh, Chad, you goon," she lamented. Then: "Hey, where are you going? The game isn't over yet."

Chad had powered off his laptop. He stooped forward even while standing.

"I'm done," he said, then trudged off to his room, softly closing the door.

Yumi returned her attention to the screen. He was never going to be good anyway.

"Your food is from Golden Peach," Yumi calls through the door. Earlier, in the restaurant, she deliberated entirely too long on what to pack for Chad. Katsu-don and japchae and goi cuon, his favorites. What had been his favorites, at least. She wonders whether he cares at all what he scarfs down every night.

She is met with the usual silence.

"Hey, you wouldn't want to play League with me by chance, would you?" Yumi asks.

She knocks. "I said," her voice rising, "your food is here there are people worried about you now are you going to thank me what is wrong with you?"

She pounds on the door. "Hey," she shouts. "How about you get off your ass and stop freeloading and start doing something with your life?"

The other side of the door remains silent.

The bag of food lands softly on the carpet.

"You are a complete loser," she mutters, then is halfway down the hall when she freezes; faintly audible: the twist of his door knob.

"Chad?"

The door, barely open—just enough to reveal a sliver of darkness—wavers slightly, as if his hand is clutching it indecisively on the other side.

"Chad." She trots back up the hallway. "Hey."

The door shuts, as if he's lost what little nerve he might have worked up. Yumi stops in her tracks.

"Chad, please. I'm begging."

She waits to see if he might open the door, then turns and walks down the hall.

For a while, until she dropped out, Yumi occasionally ran into Harold on campus: at the dining hall, at the memorial union. Yumi assumed he was crashing with friends, but he never gave her the chance to speak—her arm would raise pensively, her torso swiveling to face him as he blew past, until she was twisted backward—so she never knew whether he'd listened to her voice messages. Then she left and had Chad, and she never saw Harold again. And for years, she wondered what had become of him.

Actually, this isn't true. Like any curious person, she tracked him online and followed along on his postgraduation adventures. He backpacked around Asia and then, taking a particular liking to China, got a job teaching English in Guangzhou. There, he fell in love with a local woman. For two years they traveled the world—Auckland, Tahiti, Cape Town—recording their musings on a blog for their family and a growing fanbase. They finally settled down in Guangzhou and married and had two daughters, at which point their blogging slowed, then stopped. When Yumi stared for too long at the final photo—Harold and his family at a Japanese restaurant, celebrating the younger daughter's birthday—she fixated on his eyes, brilliant as she had ever seen, as if he could hardly fathom his luck, as if his life had turned out to be more fulfilling than he ever could have dreamed growing up in a quiet town in Ohio.

And in these moments, did she feel wistfulness and regret for a life that had slipped by, or envy and resentment for an ex-lover who was now winning in every facet of life? Yes, she did. She felt all these things. Who in her shoes wouldn't? But in these same moments, did she also feel a gentle happiness for Harold, that one of them, at least, had managed to escape the shackles of Dayton to live a life filled with adventure and wonder? No, of course not. She did not feel that way at all. Who thought like that? Certainly not Yumi. The older she became, the more exhausted she was, and the only thing preventing her from going off the deep end, she realizes, other than her will to keep Chad alive—and League, too, she can't forget about that—is her irrational fear that she, too, will one day lock herself in her bedroom and shut out the world, because in the end, how much of a difference would that make?

I decided I'm running away.

After three consecutive losses, Yumi is taking a break and has been messaging trivial things with *HellCat893*.

Yumi: Why?

HellCat893: I hate my parents. I can't deal with them anymore.

Yumi: Where?

HellCat893: I don't know. Maybe Los Angeles? That's where you live, right?

Yumi: How old are you?

HellCat893: 16 hbu?

Yumi can't remember how it feels to be sixteen, so she fills in the blank. A life not weighed down with the burden of accountability, for one. Second chances and audacity and an infinite horizon. A world rediscovered.

Yumi: Same. I'm 16.

She takes a shaky breath. Her fingers tremble as they type.

Yumi: You should totally come to Los Angeles!

HellCat893: I totally should. I've always wanted to see Hollywood and Rodeo Drive!

She closes her eyes, so hot and heavy. When she opens them, she resumes typing.

Yumi: Me too!

HellCat893: Don't you live there?

Yumi curses. I meant me too, I think you should come!

HellCat893: I saved enough for a bus ticket omg this would be so amazing. Can I stay with you for a few days?

Yumi: Just book the ticket!

HellCat893: omg yay this is the best!

Yumi: Yay you will have an amazing time!

HellCat893: Thank you for being my friend!

She powers down the laptop. The screen fades, leaving Chad's bedroom in darkness. She sits quietly in her gaming chair. She is small, and the chair is large, and she imagines this is how it feels to sit on a throne. She imagines Chad in her bedroom down the hall, lying on her bed and staring at the ceiling, and wonders if he, too, thinks of the bed as his coffin. Her stomach growls. She is starving. The other night, she served the nicest family of four. Polite and kind with Yumi and with each other, they seemed to be having the most amazing time, as if nothing could bring them more happiness than each other's company. Harmony comped them slices of tempura ice cream. Their joy was that infectious.

She sinks deeper into her chair. She imagines *HellCat893* emerging from her thirty-hour Greyhound ride, squinting into the hot California sun and tear-inducing smog. Yumi will have deleted and blocked her by then. *HellCat893* will realize there is no one to greet her, no one whose parents' home she could stay at and play League with the friend she thought she had. The day will be warm and full of promise. Screw it, she will say, and she will visit Hollywood and Rodeo Drive and post loads of photos online before she eventually finds her way back to Oklahoma, one way or another. She will stay mad at Yumi for a while, then she'll grudgingly concede that her adventure out West was exhilarating, then, over time, she'll forget Yumi completely.

Yumi covers her face. She shudders. This is what she wishes she'd done. She wishes she had grabbed Chad by the shoulders, directed him to just survive. "Run," she would whisper. She would never be as certain as she was at this moment. She would wrap her arms awkwardly around him, something that nearly resembled an embrace, before shoving him away, and she would sprint and leap into the bushes, knowing Rengar and Xin Zhao and Fizz lay in wait. In her final moments, she would see Chad racing to the edge of the forest, his lifeguard megaphone swaying like a buoy, hair fluttering in the wind, running as if his life depended on it, as if to remember his life was one worth living.

STAY BRAVE, MY HERCULES

There's a tug on my skirt. I look down.

"Hi there, young fella," I say.

"Hercules," he says.

I nod.

"I have a question," he says.

"Go on then, young man."

"Hercules," he says. "How do I become strong like you?"

I glance at his parents. They beam at their son and smile like they already know. We're at the corner of Frontierland and Fantasyland. From a distance, I hear screams at the top of Splash Mountain and calliope music from the riverboat making its way downstream. The smells of buttered popcorn and churros waft through the muggy afternoon air, reminding me that I'm hungry and that I'll be done with this shift soon.

At the far corner, Buzz and Woody ham it up for a large Chinese tour group. Cameras click, and the tourists point and shout furiously at them. Buzz and Woody take it in stride and swivel randomly and wave enthusiastically and do this jiggy kind of dance. Today, Zac is Buzz.

He's a good dude. He sees me, and without turning away from the tourists, he lowers his arm and flips me the middle finger.

I kneel down and clasp the kid's hands. He stands straight and puffs out his chest. I no longer have to think back to the script. I got this shit on lock.

All of Disney's eighteen Herculeses have nicknames; mine is Babyface Hercules. There's also Douchebag Hercules, NASCAR Hercules, the high school twins Juicehead and Jailbait, Born-Again Hercules, and everybody's favorite: Grandpa Hercules. Grandpa Hercules is literally a grandpa, and in the breakroom between shifts he brings out photos of his granddaughters, and we tell him they're beautiful, because we love him. Then one of the Jasmines or Snow Whites helps him reapply his makeup, because he needs a shit-ton.

I've been Hercules ever since I gave up my diving scholarship and dropped out of college to be with Jay. I would've come back even if he wasn't sick. But the night he called and matter-of-factly explained that it had spread to his lymph nodes and testicles and brain, I immediately packed a backpack and left the Michigan snow and drove straight to Florida.

Jay is thirty years older than I am. He warned me when we first met that something like this might happen. Bodies break down over time, he had said.

On the drive back, I replayed his last words on the phone: *I am statistically unlikely to make it to the end of the year, but these standard deviations are large, as you might expect, Jeremy. . . .* Jay always talks like that. He's an actuary, which surprises nobody.

When I pulled into his driveway that morning in yet another torrential Orlando rainstorm, my fuel tank empty and my eyes bleary and my breath reeking of gas station coffee, he walked out onto the driveway, his glasses fogged and dripping, his robe blowing against his gaunt frame as it absorbed the rain. He looked at me as if he were struggling for words, and then he said, "You just drove a little over twelve hundred miles, which by my calculations puts your average speed at—"

I flung myself onto him and kissed him. "Not fast enough," I said as I pulled him back into the house.

"I'm starving, let's grub," I said later as we lay in his bed. "And I'm done with this long-distance shit," I said. "I told my parents I'm moving in with you, and that you're not doing well."

He just kind of shook his head and looked sad.

The first thing I did after I moved in with Jay was look for a job. Aladdin and Gaston and Donald Duck train at my gym, and one day we were all talking by the water fountain, and they said they might be able to help. The next thing I knew, I was at Disney employment headquarters getting my head measured and my chest waxed under the watchful, glowering scrutiny of the casting director.

I got over myself and went all in with this job. I mean, it's not awful, and at night, after Jay falls asleep, I hop online and look for other jobs, like I promised I'd do. I get to the park an hour before my shift, and they tell me where I need to be and at what time and anything I need to be aware of. Then I get in line with the other cast members for makeup. I go to the locker room and change into costume. The casting director sometimes scrutinizes me—she calls it quality control—and checks me off on her clipboard. Then I'm out the door, squinting under the bright Disney sun. For the next three hours, I smile and hug and flex, and the best part is that I get to drop wisdom bombs on adoring crowds, even though my answers are limited to what's on script. Be strong and be brave, I say. Listen to your parents. They're not half bad.

During orientation, the casting director handed me a thick binder filled with scripts to memorize so I'd know how to stay in character for every conceivable situation. Every catastrophe here is called a situation, and every situation is covered. If lightning strikes and flambés a sixth-grade class, there's a section for what Hercules would do. When a soccer mom tries to kiss me on the lips, I'm supposed to pretend to play hard to get and then try to distract her by showering her with compliments. Hercules can be such a tease. Then when her husband tries to pick a fight with me, I'm supposed to pretend that we're actually playfighting, and then I'm supposed to run and get out of there. When a kid's being a jackass and asks a dumb question—this part I actually like—I'm supposed to twist his question into one that's more family friendly, and then from there I'll give one of my stock answers. In the end, it's all about staying on script and running and evading. I am a born natural.

The boy and his parents stare at me expectantly.

"Hercules," the boy repeats. "How do I become strong like you?"

I'm hungry and it's my break soon and the scent of those churros is slaying me, but this kid is adorable, so I squeeze his hands and gaze into his wide eyes.

"Young man, what's your name?"

He takes a deep breath and shouts, "Garen."

"Young Garen, I want you to be strong, I want you to be brave, and I want you to listen to your parents. Do you understand?"

Garen turns and looks at his parents, who seem close to combusting with pride. They reach for each other's hands and mouth the words *I understand, Hercules* at him.

Garen focuses his attention back on me. He puffs his chest out, and he shouts: "Dad wears Mom's dresses and makeup like you do."

When he sees me with my mouth agape, he attempts to clarify. "But only when Mom's not home," he assures me.

I know the absolute worst thing I can do at this moment is to look at Garen's parents, but that's what I do. Their hands are clasped, and their smiles remain plastered on, but nothing registers in their eyes. Like four vapid orbs gatewaying into an abyss. Then she shoves away his hand and looks at him with confusion, and it's like I can already see her about to say, *Honey, is that true?*, and I can already imagine him struggling to respond, and then I'm like, nah, this fool is so boned. And in this moment, the only thing running through my mind is, I'll be damned, that binder doesn't cover everything after all.

* * *

"They don't pay us enough for this shit," Zac says.

Zac and I are slumped in our chairs in the breakroom. We're still in costume.

In the far corner, Annabelle is having lunch with her daughter. In the past, as Ariel, Annabelle was legendary for how she connected with the kids. There would be a line of children with their parents snaking around the corner as they patiently waited to hug her and tell her about school and their pets. She would smile and say, "Tell me more." Then Annabelle had her daughter. When she returned from maternity leave, she had put on a little weight, and they reassigned her as a fully covered Mickey. Her Mickey headpiece sits on the table as her daughter cries and says she doesn't like to be left with cast members' childcare.

"I'm so sorry, sweetie," Annabelle says. She looks exhausted.

"So, what did you say to that family?" Zac asks.

I shrug.

Garen's mom had marched toward us and was about to yank Garen away when I stood and gently held her hand.

"Ma'am," I said.

She tried to shake my hand off. Her back and shoulders were as rigid as a springboard.

"Just let us go," she said, and her shoulders slumped, and I saw tears well in her squinting eyes.

"Can I just say something real quick to Garen?" I asked.

She hesitated, and then she tightly nodded.

I knelt down and grabbed Garen's hands once again. He looked confused and as if he might cry too. I leaned forward and spoke right into his ear.

"Young man," I said, and he whispered a tiny yes back.

"Hercules wants you to know," I said, "that no matter what happens, your dad and mom love you very much, OK?"

"OK."

"So, I want you to be brave, and I want you to be strong, and I want you to listen to everything they tell you, OK?"

"OK."

"And now," I whispered, "Hercules wants you to go give your mom and dad a big hug. Can you do that for Hercules?"

He ran to his mom and hugged her tight, and he ran to his dad, who had been standing unsurely in the background. Then they were gone, and my shift was about over, so I stood and walked back to the breakroom.

I think for a moment. "I guess I stayed on script," I tell Zac.

He stares.

"I mean the script's not half bad," I say, and he shrugs and loses interest.

Jay looks up from his spreadsheets when I come home that night. His company lets him work from home, so most nights I find him surrounded by reams of paper. He doesn't let the cancer stop him from putting in a full workday, and he's meticulous about tracking his hours.

"How was your day?" he asks.

"It was a blast," I say. "Dads getting caught lying, and kids needing therapy for the next ten years."

"So just another Disney day?" he says.

"Yep. How was yours?"

He takes off his glasses and rubs his eyes before he reaches for a stack of papers. He lifts a page off the stack.

"Jeremy," he says. "We need to talk about inheritance and insurance. I've run some initial calculations, and the projections indicate . . ."

I tune out when he uses big words, but he gets more animated as he picks up steam on his findings, and he's sexy as fuck as he incessantly taps his paper with his pen, so I strip off my shirt and straddle him.

He stops talking.

"Ah," he says.

"Let's talk about your impending death some other time," I say.

Later, I step out of the shower and find Jay curled up on the sofa. His glasses, off-kilter, are hooked onto one ear and hanging on his forehead over wisps of fine hair. He snores lightly. I stare at his face. When he's awake, he always looks as if he's worried about something, probably because he is. Worried about me, probably. He likely has months left, and the only thing he seems to have on his mind is whether I'll be OK after he's gone. It's only when he's asleep that he looks relaxed. He snorts, and traces of a thin smile form. I wonder what he's dreaming about, and that makes me smile.

I was back home with Jay for summer break when we first learned about the cancer. By then, we'd been together for two years. The prognosis was bright then, and Jay was adamant I return to college.

"I'll be cured before you come back," he said.

That night, needing to get out of the house, we went to P. F. Chang's.

"Are we celebrating anything special tonight?" our server asked.

"Just our health," Jay said gently.

"That's very sweet," the server said, smiling. She studied us, and she said, "Well you two look as healthy as—"

"It's my birthday," I cut her off. Her mouth curved into an O, and she said she'd give us a minute to look at the menu.

Jay gave me his look.

"What? Health doesn't get you free cake at P. F. Chang's," I said.

"I suppose that's true," he said.

We were subdued for most of the dinner. It was toward the end, after dessert, that I could no longer hold back.

"What if things go wrong?" I was reeling from too many apple martinis.

"Jeremy," he said. "Do you realize, statistically, how many standard deviations off we need to be to see the treatment fail?"

I said nothing.

"It's a little under three," he said. "Expressed numerically, that equates to—"

"OK. OK."

He reached over for my hand.

"I'm going to be fine, Jeremy. You must trust me, and you have to trust in the numbers."

I relented.

In the darkened room, the candle flickered over his creases and tiny orange flames reflected in the lenses of his glasses. He's all lit up in fire, I thought. And I believed. But I should have never left him.

Everybody's in a shitty mood today at the park. This happens sometimes. Some days, with no reasonable explanation, anger spreads and takes over entire sections of the park like a contagion. By midmorning, under the already scorching sun, tempers flare within families and in groups of middle school friends, Tomorrowland's Space Mountain dome standing glumly as the backdrop.

This includes Noah, the six-year-old baldheaded Make-A-Wish kid from Dayton, Ohio, who sits in his wheelchair with his arms crossed. He glares as his parents stand helplessly to his side and the swath of media photographers fumble with the cameras draped around their necks and do not take photos.

Noah's mom approaches him and places her hand on his frail shoulder. "Honey," she says, "is there anything we can do to make you happy?"

"I want to go home," he says, and the Make-A-Wish and Disney public relations people all wince.

"But sweetie," she says. "Isn't this what you wanted to do more than anything in the world? What changed?"

"Disney World sucks," he shouts, and two photographers quietly pack their cameras into their cases.

Dad is starting to unravel, and I see him approach Noah with frustration. Before I realize what I'm doing, I'm standing between Noah and his burly dad, my face lit up with a smile. I motion subtly at his dad before I kneel down and face Noah.

"Hi there, young man. You're Noah, right?"

Noah stares at my biceps with wide eyes. My physique generally has that effect on boys who worship Marvel superheroes and professional wrestlers, and I can imagine that the effect is greater on a kid as sick as Noah. He looks into my eyes shyly.

"Young man," I say. "I hear you on your discomforts. It's too hot and it's too crowded and everybody's in a bad mood."

He nods emphatically.

"So, tell me," I say. "If you could do anything right now, what would it be?"

His face brightens. "Video games," he says.

I say, "Hercules loves video games. What's your favorite?" and he shouts, "Minecraft," and I exhale in relief. That's the one game I have some knowledge of.

"That's Hercules's favorite game," I say, and he looks as though he might jump out of his wheelchair and hug me. "What are you working on right now?" I ask, and Noah smiles and closes his eyes for several moments, as though he's transported himself out of Disney and into his Minecraft world. When he opens his eyes, they are shining.

"I found a way that I can fly forever," he says.

I say, "Hercules wants to hear all about this." The photographers take their cameras back out of the cases, and as they record from a distance, Noah explains to me in a feverish pitch and with two animated hands the mechanics and items he acquires before he sprints and dives off a cliff and launches himself higher and higher into an infinite horizon—so high, in fact, he explains, that the game stops rendering his image, and he disappears entirely from the screen.

"That is very high," I agree. "But Noah," I say. "If you fly beyond the horizon and disappear, won't you miss your parents?"

"It's just a game, Hercules."

"Touché."

"Hercules?"

"Yes, Noah."

"I'm sick, you know," he says. From the corner of my eyes, I sneak a peek at Noah's parents. They stare intently at their son.

"I know," I say.

"Hercules?"

"Yes, Noah."

"Will you come to my home and play Minecraft with me?"

I say nothing.

"So we can fly forever?" he says.

I can see in his eyes that he is bracing for the inevitable no.

"I have an even better idea," I tell him as I begin to smile. He looks up. "Peter Pan's Flight is close. Have you been on that ride?"

He shakes his head.

"Hercules promises you," I say, "that riding that ride feels just like flying. How about we take that flight together, just you and me?"

He considers this for a moment and then says OK. I glance at his parents for permission, and they look like they might throttle me with gratitude, so I stand and take Noah's hand as his mom pushes his wheelchair. Behind us, the photographers and media and public relations teams quietly follow, and the crowd ahead splits to make room when they see the procession. But I have eyes and ears and heart only for Noah—script be damned—and he has me eating out of his hands as he patiently explains master-level tips on how to rule over the Minecraft domain.

A photo of me kneeling and clasping a smiling Noah's hands makes the front page of the newspaper the next morning, along with the caption "Local Hero Captures the Hearts of Boy and Disney Community."

Jay lowers the paper over breakfast. "You sure work hard for thirteen dollars an hour," he points out.

"They should promote me to management," I say crossly. I couldn't sleep last night.

"Or at least to play Gaston. Now that's a real man," Jay says as he dodges the Cheerio I flick at him. He raises the paper, and I get ready to leave for work.

The Orlando roads are slick with rain this morning, and the traffic is heavy. I've always wondered why they chose to build the Happiest Place on Earth in practically the Wettest City in the Country. I like it when it rains, though.

I stare past the wipers sweeping frantically on the windshield. Outside is a sea of gray. With every gust of wind, sheets of rain shimmer. Trees shudder. I hear the wail of sirens approaching. I pull over and stare at the ambulance as it passes and then turns, heading in the opposite direction from home. I remain parked by the curb. The sirens fade, and rain pelts the roof of the car and my heart beats furiously. I rest my eyes, and the heat radiates through my closed eyelids.

Yesterday at Peter Pan's Flight, while waving a temporary goodbye to Noah's parents and the media folk, I helped Noah step on board the suspended galleon that served as our flying ship. We settled in our seats and launched high into a dark London night. We flew over Tower Bridge and Big Ben before rising to clouds of wispy white fluff swaying under giant whirring fans made invisible behind the cloak of night sky. Below, a sea of tiny golden lights—villages of homes shining kerosene lanterns—twinkled and pulsed, as if the constellations lay not above us but below.

I looked at Noah. He was spellbound as we glided and swooped over mountain peaks and into the heart of Neverland. At one point, our galleon suddenly lifted to escape the wrath of an enormous crocodile. Noah whooped and wrapped his arms around me. I squeezed his shoulder and pointed down at the crocodile, who now held Captain Hook in his jaws.

As our galleon exited to the disembarking zone, where Noah's parents would welcome us back, Noah rested his head on my shoulder.

"How'd that feel?" I asked. "Was that just like flying or what?"

He said, "That was way better than Minecraft." I squeezed him tight before I helped him off the galleon and into his waiting wheelchair.

After posing for a final round of photos, I said my goodbyes and jogged back to my post in Tomorrowland. As I navigated between throngs of people heading to their next attraction, I imagined that it had been Jay and I flying on the galleon. Jay, being Jay, would peer over the ledge and at the city below, and he'd squint and point out, "The placement of Big Ben seems off. It should be over there." I'd tell him to shut up and enjoy the ride. He'd be silent for a moment, and then he'd look up toward the ceiling and say, "The engineering in this facility is really quite remarkable, if you stop and consider—"

"Shut up," I'd say again.

I'd close my eyes and shiver when the cold air blew over my ears. In the distance, Peter Pan and Hook's swords would whirl and clang in battle as the Darling kids cheered and whistled. Jay would cock his head and say, "Is everything OK, Jeremy?"

And I'd grip the ledge so hard that pain would shoot up my wrists, but he wouldn't see that, and I'd smile and say, "Yeah, just hungry. Let's get a turkey leg after this." And for the rest of the ride we'd stay quiet, our galleon propelling us above a dark ocean and gliding toward the exit, where sunlight would peek in from around the corner and the cast members, bored shitless, would remind us to watch our step on our way out.

DIESEL GIOVANNI

My first night performing live is also my fourth-grade teacher Erika Einhorn's sixtieth birthday. Her schoolteacher friends have dragged her here to Dayton Dix to celebrate. Neither she nor I expected to ever see each other again, yet here we are eleven years later. She sits stiffly on a folding chair center stage under the spotlight, hands folded neatly in her lap. Our forced smiles assure the boisterous crowd this is fine, this is normal. My arms wrap her in an awkward embrace, and we quietly negotiate the terms and conditions on the spot.

"You may strip down to your skivvies, Logan McMakin, but that's it," she hisses.

"Yes, Mrs. Einhorn."

"And for goodness' sake, do not rub your butt in my face."

"It's Diesel Giovanni, please."

"OK, Logan."

The crowd roars.

"Stick your schlong in her face," screams Mabel Rogerson, my seventy-two-year-old first-grade teacher at Southeast Dayton Phase Two Elementary School.

"Don't listen to her," Mrs. Einhorn says, her face pale.

"Rest assured, ma'am, I am a trained professional."

I lift my firefighter's hat and fling it carefully. It's red and it's plastic and I bought it at Party City last week. My first one cracked and broke during practice when I flung it too far.

I feel a jab of guilt when Mrs. Einhorn begins to tremble. She is even more uncomfortable than I am. My mind races for a way to soothe her and still appease the bloodthirsty crowd, especially Mrs. Rogerson, who is now standing on the table and thrusting her hips, as though to demonstrate her expectations. In the corner, the security guard eyes her warily.

It's Tuesday, what should be a quiet night, but this raucous squad of schoolteachers has upended expectations and caused our manager, Alvaro, to frantically call for backup.

"Captain Spankin'?" he says urgently, pressing a finger into his other ear. "We got a cadre of thirsty teachers. Hello? Tight Booty McSluity? Oh my god, what is she doing?"

He stares with horror at Mrs. Rogerson. She's trying to strip the shirt off the security guard, who's asked her to step off the table but now hunches forward and grips his shirttails in an attempt to stay clothed.

From the corner of the stage, his arms folded, wearing police pants and no shirt, Midnight Marcus looks at me intently. I shake my head. *I got this,* I mouth. Midnight Marcus, the veteran who has managed to gyrate and smooth-talk himself out of every conceivable catastrophic situation onstage, is a legend among us Dayton male exotic dancers.

Mrs. Rogerson has climbed back onto the table, and now she is fist pumping, and now she is raising the roof, and now oh my god she is dabbing why would she do that, and now she is demanding the security guard join her on the table, and he is doing his best not to laugh.

I position myself before Mrs. Einhorn, shielding her from the crowd, and lightly clasp her shoulders.

"She's really making this worse," she says, miserably.

"We always knew she was a nutcase," I tell her.

She looks up. "I thought she was everybody's favorite."

I shake my head. "That was you, Mrs. Einhorn," I say. "You were my favorite."

She looks doubtful. "Is that Diesel Giovanni talking? Or Logan?"

"Hey," I say. "It's me. Your Logan. Your perfect-attendance Logan."

I feel a tap on my arm. Midnight Marcus hands me a vodka tonic. I whisper thanks, and he quietly vanishes in the way he does. I proffer the drink.

"For the birthday girl. And the best damn teacher Southeast Dayton Phase Two Elementary School has ever had."

She tilts her head back and downs the whole cocktail, then gasps.

I swallow my surprise. "Better?"

She considers this. "I suppose so," she says. For the first time tonight, she meets my gaze, then smiles tightly.

Good enough. I motion at the DJ. The speakers' volume rises to a deafening blare. Aerosmith commands us, very loudly, to walk this way. With my back facing the crowd, I jerk and drop my firefighter coat to the floor. The crowd goes hog wild. I pull Mrs. Einhorn's hands to my chest.

"You sure you're OK with this?" I ask.

She takes a shaky breath. "Let's go, *Diesel Giovanni*."

Midnight Marcus nods approvingly and exits the stage. I circle the chair and stand behind Mrs. Einhorn. Facing the crowd, all of whom are cupping their hands around their mouths and hollering incomprehensible instructions, I sling my arms over her shoulders and lower my head into the crook of her neck. She shivers.

I whisper, "Time to get schooled, Mrs. Einhorn."

In my freshman year at Dayton High, I was quickly cut from the junior varsity football team, though to be fair, I was probably better suited for the cheer squad. I then joined the cross-country team, only to quit two weeks later upon discovering that long-distance running was dull. As a last-ditch attempt at redemption, I became the manager for the girls' soccer team. But when Kayla sprained her ankle in the first match of the season, I ran onto the field with the coach, tripped, and sprained my ankle, too.

"You can't be serious." The coach looked at me in disbelief.

I wailed, grasping my ankle. As the girls smiled at me with sympathy, I watched any chance at popularity evaporate into the cloudy Ohio skies.

Fia and the coach carried me off the field with embarrassing ease.

"I hope you feel better soon," Fia whispered in my ear.

My face burned hotter than my ankle.

When I recovered, I sheepishly informed the coach I wouldn't be returning, and instead I spent my afternoons over the next three years holed up in the high school weight room, secure in the knowledge that no team could cut me again. Here, quietly, I grew stronger.

In my senior year, the soccer team organized an amateur boxing night for a fundraiser. Fia, who had carried me off the field three years earlier, cornered me in the cafeteria.

"Sign up for this." She shoved the pen and clipboard at my chest.

"I can't box."

"You're the strongest guy at our school. That has to count for something."

"I don't think it does," I said.

"Sign up and I'll go on a date with you after the smoker."

I signed up before she could change her mind. Then, for the next ten days, I studied boxing online, discovering I was in way over my head. My fighting experience consisted of three months of karate when I was eight. My parents had acquiesced to my pleas and signed me up for classes. But fees kicked in at the rank of yellow belt, so when I was promoted, they yanked me out and shuttled me to the next dojo, until I exhausted all the dojos in Dayton. My four white belts were lost somewhere in the depths of my closet.

There was no way I could learn even the rudiments of boxing in time without paying for a trainer I couldn't afford. I stood before the computer, failing to mimic the instructors in the videos, who made the jabs and strikes and footwork look effortless. My only hope was that my opponent was also studying tutorials online, asking himself what he could have possibly been smoking to have agreed to this.

My prayers were answered. I was matched with Spencer Ackermann, slow and lumbering and doughy, because we were closest in weight. They set up the school gym event-style with the bleachers pulled forward and the ring at half-court. Trudging through a low sea of mist from a slate of fog machines, I climbed into the ring, initially apprehensive but less so when Spencer entered petrified, as though he was totally willing to accept defeat if it meant he could just leave. He refused to look me in the eye when we bumped gloves. I could only imagine what he had been promised.

The bell rang. We threw halfhearted jabs, with no real intention to inflict hurt. I had resigned myself to putting up a good faith fight, but after seeing the misery painted on Spencer's face like embalming cream, I quickly lost all desire to hit him, and through our classmates' crescendo of boos and insults, we acted our way through an astoundingly gentle, empathetic match. I danced around him, actually danced, a mashup of faux jabs and uppercuts and "Single Ladies" moves. Our classmates guffawed, then eventually began to cheer. Taking the cue, Spencer danced, too, though he was terrible. That only further invigorated the crowd. Grinning loopily, we cranked in circles, our relief at believing we might have dodged a terrible fate outweighing our embarrassment, until the referee mercifully put a stop to the fight.

Later that night, sitting in the back of the theater on our date, I worked up the nerve to ask Fia if she regretted signing me up.

"Why would I?"

"It probably didn't help with fundraising."

"I wasn't thinking about that when I asked."

"What were you thinking?"

I already knew the answer, and my face burned with surprise and elation and sheepishness. I gripped the armrest and my heartbeat throbbed in my fingertips.

"You can't be this dense, Logan."

“Sometimes my muscles get in the way of thinking,” I explained, and she laughed, and I laughed, and when we walked out of the theater a little past midnight, our hands clasped, smiling because the night was cool and the world felt right, I looked up and swore I could see the curvature of the dark sky, as though the universe were bending into itself just to make tonight happen.

There’s this part of my act where I whip my shirt in frenzied circles, the implication being that at any moment I will stop twirling and use it to smack my client’s butt, who I will have positioned by then on her hands and knees. Sometimes the client gets so into it that I remind them it’s just a show, and to please behave. Sometimes that excites them even more.

This is what’s supposed to happen. But Mrs. Einhorn isn’t having it.

“What in the world are you doing?” she says, resisting my attempt to lower her to the floor.

“Shhh,” I reassure her. “Diesel’s got this.”

“Logan, I have *arthritis*.”

“Oh.”

I think forward to the next part of the routine that doesn’t involve straddling the ground. I lead her back to the seat center stage as my mind races through the steps: the pivot and grind, then the faux hump, then the emotional turn with the tender embrace, then I pull them off the ground—this is the part I need to skip forward to—and then and then, oh that’s right and then I steer them back onto the ground, crap.

The crowd’s cheers dissipate, and a restless stir fills the room. Mrs. Einhorn has folded her arms.

I feel the tap on my shoulder.

“May I have this dance?” Midnight Marcus says from behind me.

Mrs. Einhorn, perking up in Midnight Marcus’s calming presence, takes his arm. I get out of their way as Midnight Marcus improvises a kind of performance-for-seniors: gentle, soothing gyrations, a shoulder massage more physiotherapeutic than sensual. At one point, Mrs. Rogerson loudly moans, “Now that there is a *Gentleman*.”

This is a *strip* club, I want to protest. I've been pushed offstage, and I catch Midnight Marcus's gaze only once. He nods sympathetically and then turns his attention back on Mrs. Einhorn.

At the end of the night, in the back room, I rub my eyes and lower my head. I can't make it through a single shift without screwing up. I can't believe I let Midnight Marcus convince me I was ready; I can't believe I let him bring me here in the first place. Shame follows, that I would so hastily shunt the blame to anyone but myself.

"It's OK, my man," a voice calls out.

I lift my head. Midnight Marcus is by my side, studying me.

"I feel like garbage," I say.

"You're going to be incredible one day," he says. "Just keep at it."

"What do I do until then?"

He smiles and places his hand on my shoulder. "What we all do. Just fake it."

Nothing made those of us destined for mediocrity more depressed than witnessing ambitious classmates escape to other states and restart their lives with a fresh scorecard. You love Dayton, I reminded myself as I scrolled through photos of them at college, posing regally with their roommates in sunlit dorm rooms, filling circular tables in cavernous dining halls, packing stadiums in matching sweatshirts and red face paint, as if Dayton had been shackling them all along.

After seven months together, it was Fia's failure to convince me to go to college that led to the first of our arguments.

"I'm happy here," I insisted.

It was the summer after we graduated from Dayton High. I lay on her bed as she crouched over her laptop and planned her move to Columbus.

"What is it about Dayton that makes you happy?" she asked.

I wasn't sure. It crossed my mind that it was like how my parents and I had had goetta for weekend breakfasts for as long as I could remember, even after we'd established none of us really cared for it. We didn't hate it.

"I'm not staying in this dump," she said. "Plus, I need to make something of my life."

So I acquiesced to her proposal that we put our relationship on hiatus—she would be very busy, she said—and we said goodbye, though we stayed in touch, regularly at first but then less so. With each text, I sensed the distance growing, as though Columbus and Dayton sat atop separate tectonic plates, gradually and irrevocably drifting apart with every slight tremor.

After Fia left, and with nothing to look forward to except for the gym, I got a job driving the train at the Fairfield Commons mall. My uniform consisted of a conductor's hat. Otherwise, I could wear whatever I wanted. In the summers, I wore a tank-top. In the winters, when all of Ohio was blanketed in snow, I wore a tank-top, too, for the surprise factor. Basically, I always wore a tank-top.

Shoppers boarded at the atrium by the food court. "All aboard!" I was to yell every two minutes. When the atrium was deserted, which was often, I would yell, "All aboard the Logan train!" I thought that was clever.

Then I slowly drove past the storefronts, the passengers calling out the stores that we passed.

"Look, sweetie," a mother said. "Hollister is having a sale."

"Ugh," the daughter said. "Literally nobody wears Hollister anymore, Mom."

I snuck a look back. The mother, who wore a Hollister shirt, looked deflated.

Fia came back to visit over her fall break. *Where are you*? she texted.

Working, I texted back, almost crashing the train into a column just past Aéropostale.

"Can you stop?" The woman in the front car leaned forward and poked my shoulder. "I'd like to get out here."

"This is not a bus service—ma'am, please stay in your seat—ma'am . . . OK sure, fine, do whatever."

Twenty minutes later, my feet propped up on the train ledge, I bolted upright when I saw Fia emerge from JCPenney and head in my direction. I leaped out of the train. We met and embraced in front of Wetzel's Pretzels in a billowing waft of yeast and cheap butter and burnt cinnamon. Her scent, so familiar, hit me like an unexpected fall storm and transported me back to Dayton High, standing beneath her umbrella by the fields on a drizzly gray afternoon, watching from the warmth of the library as the rain pummeled the pavement.

"Do you ever not wear a tank-top when driving this thing?" She smiled brightly.

"No."

"I miss seeing you," she said. "What are you doing after your shift?"

I squinted in concentration. "Today is Thursday. So back and biceps and abs."

"Oh my god, Logan."

"Unless you're up for something."

At Applebee's, over wings and grilled chicken quesadillas, I listened with fascination as Fia spoke about classes that met only twice a week and how attendance wasn't recorded, how final exams sometimes accounted for the entire grade, how students came from all over the state and other parts of the world.

"My lab partner is from Kazakhstan," she said casually, sipping her lemonade.

I couldn't imagine how they must have felt traveling all the way from—actually, I had no idea where Kazakhstan was in relation to Ohio.

She told me about the night she and her friends from her dorm floor lay out in a field on the outskirts of Columbus. They swore the faint band of light above the horizon was the Milky Way. She was doubtful, but she felt at peace, elated to have found a sense of community at this mammoth university in this new city, which until that day had felt as vast and hard to navigate as the skies above them.

"Leaving Dayton was terrifying, but I'm glad I did," she said.

"Should we get the Blue Ribbon Brownie?" I asked.

"The world is bigger than Dayton," she said.

"It's big enough for me. Want to catch a movie tomorrow?"

"I want to help you apply to college. Community college. How about Sinclair?"

"Or we can go for chili dogs."

She looked at me strangely, then said, "Text me when you're done with work."

I think I hoped she'd be the one to text first. Or maybe I was tired of her doling out advice I hadn't asked for. Or maybe I'd conceded that the gap in our ambitions had widened and couldn't be traversed. Either way, I sat in my car in the parking lot that night after my shift, my chili dog untouched and getting cold, scrolling aimlessly on my silent phone, wondering if she was still in Dayton or had already left for Columbus, wondering if her finger was also hovering over the send button. I fought back the creeping feeling that I was making yet another mistake.

One spring afternoon, mind-numbingly bored in the atrium, I saw a face I knew from the gym. The guy was with his two preschool-aged daughters, and they were boarding the train. I did a doubletake. He flicked his head up in acknowledgment. Once I got us going, I turned back and smiled and waved at the girls. They giggled shyly, and we settled into a kind of game; every few seconds, I turned and made a face, and they erupted in shrieks.

The man approached me when the ride ended.

"You're good with people," he said.

"Thanks."

"I've seen you at the gym." He squinted and examined me. "You work out hard. How do you like your job?"

I shrugged. "It pays the bills."

Actually, I lived with my parents and didn't have many bills.

"You know how to dance?" he asked.

"I guess so, sure."

"I can hook you up with a job that pays three times what I'm guessing you make here. Interested?"

"Hell yeah."

He retrieved a card from his pocket. "Call me tonight. We always need good guys."

Then he left with his girls.

Midnight Marcus, the card read. Of Dayton Dix, it read.

It's a busy, well-behaved night, a month after the schoolteacher fiasco. We rotate from the stage to the tables and back like clockwork, as if reading our customers' minds and their whims couldn't come easier. Madison is grieving a breakup, so we shower her with attention and terrible jokes. Deitra is celebrating a job promotion. After sleuthing, I casually mention, as I hook her fingers on my thong, that I also went to Southeast Dayton Phase Two, and she cries with laughter when I describe her former teachers storming into Dayton Dix and corrupting our minds. The bartender whirs and shakes and pours furiously to keep up. Tips and racy banter flow.

During break, on the lounge chair in the back room, Midnight Marcus is FaceTiming his two daughters, who are getting ready for bed. His face is awash with contentment and pride.

"Diesel," he calls out. "Come say hi."

I weave around behind the chair and wave at them, adorably nestled in one bed.

"It's the train guy!" one says, waving frenetically.

"Are you two behaving?" I ask.

They look at each other and giggle. I hand the phone back to Midnight, who blows them a kiss before he puts away the phone.

"You're a good father."

He sighs. "God knows I come up short. I dread the day they're old enough to have to reckon with their dad being a stripper."

"Thought about what you will say?"

He shrugs. "I'll tell them it's what I'm good at. I just hope that'll be enough." He stands. "Let's get ready."

I change into scrubs. I sling the plastic stethoscope around my neck and strap the surgical mask to my forehead. I squint at my reflection in the vanity mirror. I look good. Smart. Successful. Ambitious. The kind of person you show off to your parents.

Three women enter the club. My heart races. I'd recognize that face anywhere. I haven't seen or spoken with Fia since the night at Applebee's three years ago, and now here she is in Dayton Dix. I trace my fingers across the contour of my abs as the women choose a table in the middle of the room.

I run my hand through my hair, take a deep breath, and make my way toward them. She sees me approach, and then moves her attention back to her friends.

"Hey," I say when I reach them. I'm standing right by her. I wait for her to turn toward me, which she eventually does.

"I heard you might be working here," she says. Her voice is neutral, a little distant. Nothing a little stripper humor can't fix.

"I'm a doctor now," I say, clutching my stethoscope. She doesn't laugh.

The server approaches and sets down glasses of water, glances at us, then wordlessly disappears.

"So. Would you like a dance with a surgeon?"

Her friends shake their heads, but my focus is Fia.

She smiles thinly. "Maybe later."

"Fia. Come on. Please?"

Her friends glare at me, indignant. I reach for Fia's hand.

"Fia."

She pushes my hand away.

"Just stop, Logan."

I back off.

"Well, it's great to see you." I nod at her friends. "Ladies," I say. I wander off, my face burning.

Midnight Marcus approaches me. "What was that about?"

"What do you mean?"

"You lost your groove the second they walked in." He squints, then grimaces. "You know them? Got the hots for one of them?"

I don't answer.

He shakes his head. "What did I tell you, my man? You're gonna have to do better than this."

He walks toward their table, flashing a wide smile. I see him extend his arms, embracing the air between them. I see them relax. A moment later, they laugh. Fia points at the empty chair inquisitively. He bows gracefully and sits down. He motions to the server, who is instantly at their side, holding his pen and pad.

I back into a corner and sit there, hidden in darkness, where the club lights fail to reach. Laughter peals from their table.

"Oh, Midnight!" Fia's friend cries, hand clutching at her heart.

Midnight and Fia stand. Fia takes Midnight's hand and follows him to the stage. The DJ switches to a jazz number, and I slump deeper into my seat. They sway in each other's arms, as though at a prom in a high school gym. Fia looks in my direction. For a moment, I could swear her eyes are filled with sadness. Then Midnight whispers into her ear. She throws back her head and laughs. She leans her head into his chest as he holds her.

I hide my face.

About a year after high school, on a particularly dead night at the mall, I sat in my seat on the train, counting down the minutes to the end of my shift. I sensed motion behind me, and I realized somebody was in the front car. It was Spencer, the guy I had boxed. I wasn't sure how long he'd been sitting there.

"Hey, Spencer," I said.

"Hey, Logan."

We sat there, neither of us having any idea what to say. Eventually, with nobody else boarding, I started the train, and I drove us in an endless loop through the deserted corridors. We passed one empty store after another, the associates standing around like mannequins. This place was doomed.

"Logan."

"Yo."

"Why you didn't you knock me out in the smoker?"

I turned around without slowing the train. "What?"

He shrugged. "Everybody knew the fight was yours. I mean, look at me. Why didn't you take the win?"

I didn't hit him, I thought, because it wouldn't have mattered. People like Spencer and me, we were destined to be life's afterthoughts. That night in the ring, as we locked eyes, I saw, behind his terror and dread, something like rage, or self-hatred, and I couldn't tell which, but I understood why it was there, and I felt I would never know somebody as deeply as I knew him then.

I didn't tell him that. I didn't say anything. I only sat there, watching the stores blur into one indistinguishable retail space, in this mall not unlike any other mall in the region, surrounded by vast swaths of empty parking lot, the Olive Garden with its endless breadsticks bordered by the highway, where the clouds above, as though by their own volition, chose to hang around long after they had worn out their welcome.

SURVEILLANCE (I)

Emerick Schuster's body aches in the final hours of his shift at Let's Fly!, but ever the professional, he conceals his fatigue and doles out enthusiastic words and high-fives. Seventy-three-year-old Mabel Rogerson is next. She is petite, and Emerick has fit her in a child's skydiving suit and helmet. The orange goggles cover half her withered face.

"Are you ready, Mrs. Rogerson?" Emerick shouts over the roar of the wind tunnel.

He is fond of his former first-grade teacher at Southeast Dayton Phase Two Elementary School. So far it has been uneventful with this group of eight teachers, who'd booked the standard flight package. They'd been attentive and courteous during instructions, enduring his stock flight jokes like champs.

He frowns. Mrs. Rogerson has latched onto the ledge rail, her face etched with terror.

"You can do this, Mabel," Erika Einhorn exclaims, though she herself has yet to take her turn, so her words feel a little dampened with uncertainty. She places her hand on Mabel's shoulder. Mabel snarls, and Erika withdraws her hand. *I'm sorry I'm sorry,* she mouths, then gestures at Emerick helplessly. Emerick stoops down.

"Mrs. Rogerson," he says. "I can lower the wind strength, so you'll be barely off the ground. In fact, you'll be able to reach down and touch the floor, if you want to."

Mabel's arms are shackled to the rail. "You can do that?"

"Of course."

Emerick motions at Ace, the wind operator behind the plexiglass, jerking his hand downward. Ace gives a thumbs-up, and the roar of the wind diminishes.

Mabel hesitates, then unlatches herself from the rail and clasps Emerick's hand. He leads her to the wind tunnel while the other teachers applaud. She looks up—she reaches no higher than his sternum—and waves bravely at her friends.

Emerick motions again at Ace. *Less*, he mouths, his finger pointing down. Ace obliges. Emerick is one of the most knowledgeable flight instructors here at Let's Fly!, and if he says less wind, then it shall be so.

Emerick steps into the wind tunnel first and beckons Mabel. She takes a breath and gingerly steps inside. She closes her eyes and raises her arms, as though to surrender to the Lord. Emerick places one hand on her shoulder, another on her waist, leads her to the center, and carefully lowers her into position.

The surge of wind lifts her off her feet, propelling her body. She is flying. She extends her arms and legs. She is a condor. She is Superwoman. She cries out in wonder.

"You're doing it," Emerick shouts. And though Mabel is no higher than Emerick's knees, he crouches way down, feeling a twinge in his back, and adjusts her torso so that she is comfortable.

"I'm flying! Whee!" Mabel laughs, and, seeing her exhilaration, her friends standing outside the glass cannot help but feel a burst of emotion.

"Higher! Higher!" Mabel cries, and when Emerick asks if she's sure, she shouts, "Yes, yes, higher!"

"OK!" Emerick motions to Ace and sweeps his hand up.

Moments earlier, Ace's phone buzzed, a new text. His fingers froze. It was from Crystal, who'd moved out of his studio apartment two months ago. He hasn't been able to think of anything or anybody else since then. Holding his breath, he opened the text. Three words.

I miss you

He breathed out. He'd been praying for this text every day, and here it was, finally and actually, here on his phone. His heart soared.

So when he sees Emerick from the corner of his eye motioning at him to adjust the dial a little, he's distracted, imagining what will surely be a passionate reconciliation with Crystal, and he twists the knob to maximum power.

Mabel is instantly catapulted to the top of the wind tunnel, twenty feet up, mere feet from the ceiling. Her friends gasp and cover their mouths.

"Maaaabel!" Mrs. Einhorn shrieks, thrusting her arms high in the air.

"Help!" Mabel shouts from above, barely audible over the rush of wind. "Help me at this very moment!"

Emerick leaps and grabs for Mabel's legs, though they're separated by an enormous expanse.

"Ace, what the hell?" he yells. "Turn that down!"

Oh my god oh my god oh my god, a panicking Ace mouths behind the plexiglass. Emerick sees him reach for the dial and twist it, and he knows what will happen next. He braces himself and thrusts his arms out in a cradle.

Mabel crashes down, squawking like a smushed cat. Emerick steps to the left, then raises his arms and catches her. He swings her to one side and plops her safely onto her feet. Ace has shut off the wind, so this is met with a stunned silence. Erika Einhorn has begun to cry.

"Are you OK, ma'am?" a shaken Emerick asks.

After finding her footing, a smile creeps onto Mabel's face. Her heart pumps life and adrenaline and vigor through her trembling body. She is exhilarated. This is the most fun she has had in decades. She wags her finger at Ace.

"You're a bad, bad boy," she admonishes him.

Ace squeaks behind the plexiglass, terrified and relieved and surprised to realize he's still thinking of Crystal. He is happy that Mrs. Rogerson is safe, but he is certain he will get laid tonight, and he is very, very happy about that.

The next day, Emerick walks in on his son, Reid, having sex with his secret boyfriend. A building-wide mechanical failure at Let's Fly! sent Emerick home early. For a moment, Emerick, who until now was not aware that Reid even had a boyfriend, is hurt that Reid had never mentioned anything, and then he considers the possibility that maybe Reid did tell him and Emerick forgot, and this really concerns him, so he says nothing and clears his throat.

"Dad, I can explain," Reid says in the ensuing silence.

The boyfriend has dived under the covers. His arm protrudes, probing like a tentacle, and comes upon a pair of jeans, snatching them. Emerick and Reid observe his outline thrash as he wrestles them on. The jeans are Reid's, several sizes too small.

Standing in the doorway, Emerick, who couldn't care less who Reid shags, is curious what excuse his son could possibly come up with, so he says, "Go on then."

"He's. Um." Reid panics. "He's-paying-me-for-my-body."

The boyfriend's head shoots out. "*What*? You ho, you know that's not true."

"It totally is," Reid snaps, red-faced, eyes pleading with his boyfriend, but Emerick, who musters all of his self-control to refrain from laughing, knows that any chance for collusion between these two disappeared the moment his beautiful, lying son blamed his poor boyfriend.

"I'm starving," Emerick announces. "Are you fellas hungry?"

They are, despite their sullenness. At eighteen, they are always ravenous.

"I'm Reid's dad," Emerick says to Reid's boyfriend.

“I’m Hannon,” he says, eyeing his shirt on the floor, out of reach.

At Applebee’s, Reid and Hannon’s moods improve. After they’ve devoured platters of fiesta lime chicken and oriental chicken wraps, Emerick begins prying.

“I just want to know you guys aren’t getting any grief at school.”

Emerick realizes this is not the same Dayton High he’d attended two decades ago, but this is his son, and he can never be too sure, and he likes the way Reid and Hannon interact. He sees how Reid’s eyes soften when Reid looks at Hannon.

Reid shrugs. “No one really knows about us,” he says.

“OK,” Emerick says. “And does this—” and here he hesitates. He clears his throat. “Do you still intend to go through with your plans for after high school?”

After months of torturous deliberation, Reid has decided to enlist in the Air Force. He’s scheduled to leave for Lackland in five weeks.

“Of course, Dad. Why wouldn’t I?”

“OK, great.”

Emerick hopes he masked his disappointment. Given their finances and Reid’s grades, both of which are heavily underperforming, they know this is perhaps Reid’s best chance at making something of his life, though everything about it makes Emerick sad. But what will sadden him more is if Reid ends up stuck in Dayton with a dead-end job like his own. Even still, he often imagines the scenario in which Reid changes his mind and stays here, maybe working with him at Let’s Fly!, and in these moments, he feels a surge of longing and hope.

“*I’ll* join you at Applebee’s any time, sir,” Hannon says, as if reading Emerick’s mind.

“Huh?”

“I mean if you ever want company after Reid leaves,” Hannon says quickly.

Emerick smiles. “I appreciate your kindness,” he says, and he means it. He wonders if he looks lonely already.

* * *

Three weekends later, Hannon asks Emerick if he wants to join Reid and him for their trip to the state fair in Columbus.

"If you're not busy, of course," Hannon says when Emerick and Reid look at him in surprise.

Emerick is never busy outside of work. He sneaks a glance at Reid, who agrees cheerfully.

"I'm leaving soon," Reid says. "I'd love to spend as much time with you both as I can."

Reid and Hannon were still children the last time either of them visited the fair, and they chatter excitedly on the drive to Columbus, recalling the thrill of the water gun race, the pirate ship that swung them high into the sky, the impossibly large mounds of cotton candy. When they arrive, they head straight for the Crazy Mouse coaster, where Reid and Hannon take the front seat. Emerick sits in the back. Hannon shrieks in terror from the moment the coaster begins its series of unbanked turns.

"No, we are *not* going to die," Reid yells over the roar of the coaster and Hannon's screams. "Get ahold of yourself!"

Hannon does not get ahold of himself, and Reid resorts to lowering his head and covering his ears. Emerick leans forward and offers Hannon his hand, who grabs it, holding on for dear life. A wave of familiarity and sympathy wash over Emerick: familiarity because his customers at Let's Fly! often display a similar fear, and sympathy because no person should ever feel this way.

At the exit, Hannon stumbles out of the coaster car, leaning on Reid for support.

"No more scary rides," he blubbers, and Emerick and Reid think if he considered that scary, they'll be shooting squirt guns and eating corn dogs for the rest of the day.

They take a different approach to thrill seeking and head for the Haunted Mansion, though from the outside, it looks less like a mansion and more like a battered shipping container. There's rust on the tracks and the walls, and what really scares Emerick is the thought of Reid or Hannon contracting tetanus.

This time, Emerick takes the front seat, Reid and Hannon the back. The cart lurches ahead on the dilapidated track, and they pass through swinging doors into darkness. Hannon screeches good-naturedly when the cart swivels to reveal a featureless face. From there, the ride descends into monotony, and Reid and Hannon go quiet. Emerick considers stirring things up and jumping out of the cart and accosting them around the next corner, but then thinks maybe they're enjoying a private moment, which reminds him that Reid and Hannon will have to say goodbye to each other soon. Emerick wishes, more than anything, for his son to enjoy these final days in Ohio. He tells himself to stop worrying over Reid's safety once he joins the Air Force. His friends who are military parents have dismissed his concerns. Reid will be fine, they've said. The Air Force will keep him healthy and busy and well-fed.

A flash of red light in the next room illuminates a scowling ogre. Emerick chuckles. He is less sure that he will be fine. On Emerick's bad days at work, when his shift is filled with insufferable customers, he comes home and finds Reid sprawled out on the living room floor, absorbed in his video games; simply being in close proximity to his son makes his blood pressure drop. Soon it'll only be him. He'll come home from work, and the apartment will be empty. He could date again—he *should*—but for the last eighteen years, his sole focus has been raising Reid, and he has long forgotten how romantic commitments work. He knows that now people meet romantic partners online. He wonders if the women online will see him as not unlike this ogre: faded and outdated and trying too hard to impress.

"Hang in there, buddy," Emerick says, nodding at the ogre, before they move on down the tracks.

Imagining his future, Emerick is hit with a jolt of loneliness. An ache fills the cavity of his chest. So he's surprised when a hand squeezes his shoulder as they turn the final corner out of the Haunted Mansion, sunlight flooding their squinting eyes. He turns and sees Hannon smiling at him.

"That wasn't terrifying," Hannon says.

"No, it wasn't," Emerick agrees.

Emerick figures this is a good time to give Reid and Hannon some time alone, so he excuses himself for a couple hours and says he'll meet them at the food court.

On his own now, Emerick passes pedestrians shuffling between rides. Up ahead, a crowd has gathered around a mechanical bull. A thin man, resplendent in his ten-gallon hat and shiny boots, leaps onto the bull. The crowd quiets. They know he means business. The bull begins to spin, and sure enough, the man easily handles its gyrations with swagger, releasing one hand into the air and finger-pistoling the crowd. The bull's swerves intensify, but the man shifts his weight from one side to the other, comfortably maintaining his balance. The crowd applauds.

The bull slows, the whirr of its engine diminishing before stopping completely. The crowd goes silent. Off to the side, the operator slaps futilely at the buttons, then lifts her hands and shrugs.

The man squints, then taps the bull's foam flank.

"Slap it harder!" a woman calls out.

The man cocks his head and raises his arms in confusion when the bull still fails to move.

Suddenly, the whirr of the engine returns, and the bull bucks violently and flings the man high in the air. The crowd gasps. The man screeches before landing clumsily on a mess of foam blocks. The bull stops once again.

Emerick feels sorry for the man, and it all reminds him of the time Mrs. Rogerson was shooting into the air at Let's Fly!, so he continues down the street. He takes a seat on a bench. Above him, sky gliders whirr as they transport couples from one end of the fair to the other. Fragrances of citron and vanilla and sweet kettle corn waft through the air. A breeze surfs through his hair. He shivers. It's a gorgeous day.

"We're flying! Whee!" a young girl above cries, sandwiched between her youthful parents.

When he was young, Reid would beg Emerick to take him to Let's

Fly! on Emerick's days off. Emerick happily obliged. Reid suited up, and they waited for an empty wind tunnel, and then off Reid went, his arms and legs splayed like he was riding a flying carpet, his baby cheeks flapping in the rush of wind. They went one Halloween, with Reid dressed as Ironman. After heated negotiations regarding safety and protocol, Reid was allowed to retain his full costume but swapped out the Ironman helmet for a skydiving one. After an extended flight, Reid deftly landed and pulled off his helmet. His eyes sparkled so intensely Emerick felt his heart would explode.

"How was that, son?" he asked.

"This is the best day of my entire life," Reid said solemnly.

It was probably the best day of Emerick's entire life, too.

Emerick watches families amble by, their hands linked, their laughter in sync. An elderly couple shuffles past at a glacial pace, but their smiles are carefree. From the other direction, four fraternity brothers from Ohio State meander in matching sweatshirts and baseball caps. They don't look much older than Reid. Emerick wonders if these kids realize how fortunate they are to be in college at all. The elderly couple notices the letters on their sweatshirts and flags them the kids down, and the six of them chat comfortably and familiarly, as if they've been friends all along.

Emerick checks his watch. He wonders what Reid and Hannon are up to. Wherever they are, he hopes they're enjoying this beautiful day. He hopes Reid isn't worrying about his future. *Leave that part to your dad, Son,* he thinks.

And as though by way of answer, he hears Reid call out, "Hey Dad!" from above. He looks up and sees Reid and Hannon sailing by and waving at him.

He laughs. "Fellas," he says, and his heart is full and warm. He watches them disappear in a line of trailing gliders. He smiles. Of course they would choose to ride the sky glider.

The day has come. Reid's packed bag sits by the front door. He's leaving behind virtually everything. The Air Force has made clear he should bring very little: two days' worth of socks and underwear, toothpaste, deodorant. No magazines. No jewelry, not like he has any. Emerick has taken the day off from work to drive him to the airport in Columbus. He's already looking forward to the day he'll pick Reid up at the airport, whichever holiday that is. He hopes it comes soon. He imagines Reid appearing through the airport security exit, no longer a boy, his body filling out his fatigues, his eyes weary and wise and displaying the first sign of creases when he smiles, as though he's experienced more in several months in the Air Force than in all his years growing up in Dayton.

When Reid and Hannon emerge from his bedroom, Reid's expression is inscrutable. Hannon wipes his red eyes.

Emerick stands from the couch. "You fellas ready?" he asks.

He himself is not. Nothing could have prepared him for this day.

They aren't ready, either. Emerick picks up Reid's bag. He is struck by how light it is, but he reminds himself that the Air Force will take good care of his boy.

It is early, and there are few cars on the road. They are silent in the truck. Emerick resists the urge to start up conversation. He'd like to fill the space with the sound of his son's voice, but he lets him be. Emerick, in his shoes, would want to be left alone.

Reid breaks the silence. "Hey Dad? Can we swing by Let's Fly!?"

Emerick can't recall the last time Reid wanted to go. He checks his watch. He has building keys and free reign. They don't open for a couple hours. The plan had been for a leisurely breakfast on the way to Columbus, but perhaps this was a better use of their time.

"You want to get one last flight in?" he says.

"*I'm* not doing it," Hannon says. "I will die."

"I'll teach you one of these days," Emerick says.

"He's a damn good teacher," Reid says.

As Reid changes into his jumpsuit, Emerick boots up the building lights and thermostat and wind system. He enjoys opening Let's Fly!, which he's done hundreds of times. The building is wired mostly with incandescent lights, and in the winter, when it's still black outside, watching the room emerge from darkness and feeling the cold cede to the first tendrils of warmth makes him think of the world being reborn.

In a burst of inspiration, Emerick realizes Reid hasn't experienced virtual reality skydiving, a technology Let's Fly! has just started offering. Emerick rushes into the office and retrieves a pair of goggles. When he returns, Reid is waiting by the wind tunnel. Hannon has taken a seat close by. Reid looks up curiously.

"What's that?"

"Put these on," Emerick says. "You're in for one last treat."

Emerick stands at the computer screen. When the options load, he hovers the mouse for a moment and then selects *Swiss Alps*. He enters the wind tunnel to help Reid fall into position. Soon Reid is hovering midair, and he gasps when the scenery appears in his goggles. Emerick has experienced *Swiss Alps* many times, and he knows what Reid is seeing.

"You like that, Son?" he murmurs, and though his words are swept away by the wind, Reid's smile is the only answer he needs.

Reid extends his arms, just as he did ten years ago in his tiny Ironman costume.

"This is *awesome*," Reid yells, and his son's joy makes him feel like he is the best father in the world.

He knows Reid needs no help, but Emerick places his hands on Reid's arched, swaying figure. Emerick closes his eyes and feels the rush of cool wind on his face. He only vaguely hears Reid's excited cries, as if his son is somewhere far away. He imagines his son soaring through the Alps, through the freezing country air, but Reid is Ironman, impervious to the elements, safe from harm, the perfect airman. And now Emerick's gliding through the jutting Alps, too. Trees are tiny specks. Entire forests disappear. He soars into a blanket of cumulus clouds and tastes the cool, wet drops of condensation. Above the clouds, he sees an ocean of billowing white as he ascends into a vast sky painted a beautiful pink. He can't tell if the sun is rising or setting.

II.

SOLITUDE

SURVEILLANCE (II)

Airman First Class Reid Schuster of Dayton, Ohio, sensor operator for a fleet of remotely piloted aircraft at Creech Air Force Base in Indian Springs, Nevada, is celebrating his twenty-second birthday at the Phoenix, the gayest bar in all of Las Vegas, when, exiting the men's room, he bumps into seventy-six-year-old Mabel Rogerson, his first-grade teacher. His damp hands freeze on his pants mid-wipe.

"Oh my god Mrs. Rogerson how is this even happening," he blurts out.

Mrs. Rogerson shrieks and hugs Reid, though she reaches just to the top of his chest, even wearing heels. A purple boa snakes across her shoulders, hanging nearly to the ground, and she rocks a tidy orange-and-white floral print dress from the 1970s. She looks like she's belonged at the Phoenix her entire life, while Reid still feels intimidated and out-of-place here, *here* referring to both a space and a concept larger than the Phoenix.

"But why are you here?" Reid asks weakly.

Mrs. Rogerson lifts her arm as though to deliver a karate death chop. "I've come to give you a Vegas spanking, Reid. Bend over."

"What?"

"Fear not! I jest. In fact, a dear friend is celebrating his fiftieth birthday." Mrs. Rogerson brightens. "And he wanted to celebrate here, so *here* we are." She raises her palms toward the ceiling, an amalgam of praising the Lord and raising the roof and dismissing the surreality of it all.

"You came all the way here for a friend's birthday?" Reid asks.

Mabel clucks. "When you get to my age," she says, "you do everything you can for the people who matter to you. Anyway, what brings *you* here?" She twirls one end of her boa. "Other than to ogle these gorgeous men." She sighs. "Although that's reason enough."

"It's my birthday, too," Reid mumbles, but before he can finish, Mrs. Rogerson shrieks again and seizes his arm and pulls him through the sea of men toward the bar.

"Move it! Hot birthday boy coming through," Mrs. Rogerson hollers over the din.

The crowd parts obediently.

"Mrs. Rogerson, please stop."

"I shall never. Excuse me, boys, coming through, thank you. Now *you* two behave."

"Oh god, Mrs. Rogerson."

"I *know*. Come now."

At the bar, Mrs. Rogerson orders Reid a flight of colorful vodka shots and slides the glasses toward him.

"Happy birthday." She pats his shoulder. "It's been a pleasure knowing both you and your father."

A jolt of homesickness rips through him at the mention of his father. He raises a glass. He tilts his head back and shoots it, the vodka sluicing down the back of his throat, then reaches for another.

Mrs. Rogerson ignores Reid's grimace and excuses herself, tells Reid she must return to her friend.

"You're grown up now," she chides him. "Use your powers for good, OK?"

They embrace for a final time, and then she is gone.

Back at his table, Reid reunites with his friends. Dallas and Mohammed work as blackjack dealers at an off-Strip casino, and they'd been snogging and taking sips of the Lagavulin scotch they got for

Reid's birthday. A year earlier, Dallas and Mo had stumbled upon a cowed Reid—still new to the city—alone in a corner of the Phoenix clutching his seltzer as though it were holy water, and they soon treated him like he was their younger brother. Mo and Dallas had met years before, in Provo, where they got caught making out at Mormon summer camp, then fled south to Las Vegas the day after high school graduation, never once looking back.

Now, they look past Reid, waving tentatively. Reid sees a tall shadow descend on the table.

"Look who's finally here," Dallas says, his voice high and forced.

Reid's heartbeat quickens, and then Arjun squeezes his shoulder so hard it hurts. Reid tilts his head back and kisses Arjun, who grunts. Arjun has changed out of his work uniform into jeans and a tank-top, displaying his muscled physique. Reid is still rail-thin, unable to gain any weight and too self-conscious not to wear layers of clothing.

"You should have waited for me to open the Lagavulin," Arjun says, snatching the glass that Mo hands him.

The three murmur apologies.

"I'm kidding," Arjun says.

Their laughter dies down almost as quickly as it starts.

Arjun downs the shot, then wraps an arm around Reid and draws him closer.

"Happy birthday, kid," he says.

Reid submits to Arjun's strength. He lays his hand over Arjun's stomach, feels it rumble.

"You haven't eaten?" Reid says. "I'll get you something."

"I need a steak quesadilla and onion rings," Arjun says.

Mo stands. "I'll get it," he says, brightly. "Let you two have some quality time."

"Reid will get it," Arjun says, and Mo sits down stiffly.

Reid smiles reassuringly at Mo and stands up. As he wades through the swarm of sweaty bodies, he fights off the feeling that he is tired and that he doesn't really want to be here anymore. On most nights, he's intoxicated by Arjun's displays of dominance, but tonight something feels off-kilter, as though he wishes Arjun would at least attempt to be civil with him and his friends. He thinks of Hannon back in Dayton, who, despite his occasional penchant for hysterics, didn't once treat Reid like he was inferior. And he thinks of his father, the most levelheaded person he knows, and how he wishes he hadn't taken for granted their time together. Running into Mrs. Rogerson tonight has made him feel homesick for Dayton, though he does his best to push away that feeling, too.

When he reaches the bar, he's forgotten which quesadilla Arjun wanted. Was it steak or chicken? Panicking now, he also can't remember if Arjun wanted French fries or onion rings. He goes ahead and orders all four, figuring he'll eat what Arjun doesn't. Reid should try to gain weight anyway.

He balances the tray of food as he pushes through the throng. He emerges from the crowd and halts when he sees Arjun standing by their table, facing off against an equally burly man. Arjun's chair is on the ground, and their taut faces nearly touch as they yell furiously, though Reid knows Arjun isn't listening to what the other man says. A woman is trying to pull the other man back, but he doesn't budge. Dallas and Mo stand behind Arjun, arms crossed, unwilling or afraid to attempt to restrain him. The bottle of Lagavulin on the table is mostly empty. Reid pieces together why Arjun is throwing a tantrum.

In an instant—so quick that to Reid it's a blur—Arjun cocks his fist and strikes the man, who sprawls backward and knocks the woman onto the ground. Reid isn't surprised at the force Arjun is capable of, but he is surprised that this is happening at all. He'd been hoping Arjun would behave tonight.

"What the hell?" Reid yells as Arjun draws his arm back again, but two hulking security guards have materialized, and they wrench Arjun away and drag him toward the exit. Arjun, shouting curses, is swallowed by the crowd.

"He drank too much?" Reid asks Dallas and Mo.

Dallas looks down at the table, and Mo stares into the crowd.

"Of course he did," Reid says.

“The other guy bumped him by accident,” Mo said. “But you know Arjun. I’m sorry, Reid. The Lagavulin was for you. Anyway. You should go make sure he’s OK.”

Mo is right. Tonight is done for, and Reid is a little relieved.

“Happy birthday, beautiful,” Dallas says wistfully, then embraces him, as does Mo, and for the final time tonight, Reid wades through the crowd toward the entrance. The doors close behind him, muffling the pulsing music. He looks to the right, to the left. No Arjun. He scours the streets, one endless block after another. He knows that Arjun will be fine—he has never known him to not be fine—so he calls an Uber after searching for twenty minutes. Reid will report to work in nine hours, and he is exhausted.

Back in Dayton, Emerick Schuster is sprawled out on a mint floral couch, watching twitchy video tapes of Reid he shot with a camcorder in a time when phone cameras did not yet exist. The living room lights are off, the blinds are drawn, and Emerick’s face is awash in the green glow that radiates from the television. Here is Reid, still a toddler, in the backyard dodging the arc of water from the sprinkler and shrieking, then dashing to Emerick and tugging on his shirt. A moment later, he poops in his diaper and looks up proudly at Emerick. Here is Reid a few years later, on his first day of preschool, tearfully waving goodbye and asking if they’ll ever see each other again. Emerick had nearly shut off his camcorder and flung Reid back in the car and driven them straight home.

Reid has been gone for three years. For three years, every car that passes at night jolts Emerick awake. Each morning, he wakes up groggy, disoriented. It takes him a moment to remember that Reid is not sleeping in the next room. He hates how quiet the house has become. He hates to admit he is lonely. Last week, he signed up for a bowling league, and he hates that.

Everything is great, is what he texts when Reid asks how he’s doing. Hearing the amazing things Reid is up to—the parts Reid can disclose, anyway—confirms his son is destined for something larger than the sum total of Emerick's life, and this makes it infinitely more bearable that his own ship has sailed.

Here is Reid during his first-grade graduation. Reid is all smiles, until he trips on the stage and bursts into tears. And here is Mabel Rogerson, his teacher—Emerick's, too, way back when—rushing to lift him back to his feet and—since why not—grabbing his hands and engaging him in a kind of ring-around-the-rosy, which further embarrasses Reid. Something about the graininess of the video makes Reid and Mabel look timeless. Emerick was twenty-three when he recorded this, nearly Reid's age now, and this realization takes his breath away.

The other day at the grocery store, in the pasta aisle, he heard someone call out, "Mr. Schuster?" and when he looked up, he saw Hannon approaching unsurely. Emerick extended his hand, then changed his mind and scooped Hannon into a hug.

"How is Reid doing these days?" Hannon asked when they'd exchanged pleasantries. Reid hadn't told his dad that they were no longer together.

Emerick thought carefully. "He doesn't tell me much," he said.

"I'm still around if you want an Applebee's partner," Hannon said as they parted, looking so starved for company that Emerick briefly forgot about his own solitude.

Tomorrow, after work, Emerick and Stacey will have dinner at Fleming's Prime. They've been together for just over seven months after meeting at Let's Fly!. Stacey is a law professor at the University of Dayton. She lives in Pheasant Hill and drives a BMW and dresses like she lives in New York or Paris. She is brilliant and well-read and has complex opinions about the countries that Reid's drones surveil, and it can take her a long time to fully explain these views, so Emerick no longer brings up Reid and his drones.

They will order wine and Bibb lettuce salads and desserts that are set aflame, and Stacey will pay. She will insist it isn't a problem. He'd be fine with Texas Roadhouse, but he keep this to himself.

Here they are, on the television, at the state fair in Columbus. Reid, in a kiddie car attached to a revolving spoke, appears around the curve. He waves excitedly at the camera. He waves again when he reappears moments later. And then again. A happy reunion every twelve seconds. That day, when the ride ended and Reid skipped over the platform back to him, Emerick felt something that resembled grief.

"Do you want to go again?" he asked Reid, but his son pulled him toward the next ride.

He's incredibly fortunate that Stacey is even interested in him. He tries to speak in more complete sentences these days, and he's more careful about his attire outside the house. He sometimes wonders whether Stacey regards him as a kind of project, not that he's against self-improvement, of course.

Here's the clip that Emerick meant to record over. It's Reid's birthday, and when Emerick asks him what he's wishing for, Reid hesitates and says, reluctantly, "I wish I had a mom." Emerick struggles to come up with a response and in the end remains silent. Reid's gaze is downcast, the candles on the cake flickering before him, and it is as if Reid were feeling guilty for speaking his mind, and that's what hurts Emerick the most. Later that night, Reid crawled into Emerick's bed and said, "You're the best dad in the world," and for a little while that made him feel better.

He mutes the television, then rolls over on the couch.

"Happy birthday, Son," he mumbles, then closes his eyes.

The screen is flashing the white-and-gray test pattern when he wakes up in the middle of the night. He switches the television off, then closes his eyes again. He remembers he must iron his slacks and shirt for dinner tomorrow, which, at the moment, doesn't feel worth the effort.

The following night at Creech Air Force Base, in the cockpit—a large, converted metal container—twenty-eight-year-old pilot Captain Arjun Joshi, his gaze fixed on the panel of screens before them, expertly steers the drone over the sparkling Persian Gulf. Reid, Arjun's sensor operator, sits to his right and controls the drone's camera. Arjun's thick forearms rest on the steering yoke at the edge of Reid's vision, and

Reid can't help but worry that Arjun is angry at him. Arjun hasn't mentioned the previous evening. In fact, he has barely acknowledged Reid's existence—and though this is more or less to be expected while they are at work; Reid is an enlisted airman and Arjun is an officer—Reid doesn't think it has to be as austere as this. He wants to confirm that Arjun is fine. But asking this would anger Arjun, even if they weren't at work. Arjun would think Reid was questioning his manhood. So Reid focuses on the screens.

Thirty-two-year-old Tarek Ibrahim, suspected financier and mastermind of the bombing of a military base two years ago, which resulted in the death of twelve American soldiers, is knocking back a bottle on the bow of his yacht fifteen miles off the coast of Bahrain. They've been surveilling Tarek for twelve days, during which time Reid has learned that Tarek really enjoys his libations. Dressed in board shorts and a hoodie, Tarek looks every bit the wealthy playboy, though Reid knows he is not. A breeze sweeps over the yacht, ruffling Tarek's hair.

Tarek's daughter emerges from the cabin. Wiry and lanky, like her father, she wears a pink Dora the Explorer t-shirt and purple Crocs. Her cheeks are streaked with tears.

"Zoom on target," Arjun says.

Other than a pale bruise on his cheek, hardly visible in the dim cockpit lighting, he displays no signs of a hangover or any side effects from what happened last night. Reid wonders if Arjun feels a smidgen of remorse for cutting his birthday night short. No, Reid thinks, it's unlikely. Arjun has never once apologized to him. Reid feels himself get simultaneously irritated and horny.

Reid twists the knobs, and Tarek's pixelated face enlarges on the screens. He's drinking a Macallan. Tarek's eyes crinkle as he greets his daughter. She presents her stubbed thumb, which he clasps with both hands, then smothers with kisses. The wind rustles the tails of Tarek's shirt. He wipes her smudged cheeks.

Reid leans forward. Now Tarek blows raspberries on his daughter's thumb. A smile breaks out on her face. He pats her shoulder, and she shuffles back into the cabin. Tarek pours himself another glass. Reid imagines himself on the yacht, how it would be silent except for the sway of the ocean and the rush of the wind, no land in sight, just water and sky, salt and spray.

Arjun snorts. "That girl better enjoy her time with Daddy. In a week she won't have one."

Reid looks up, surprised. He's relieved that Arjun has said something that resembles the start of a conversation. "You got the orders?"

Arjun shrugs. "It'll happen. We've been on this motherfucker for weeks."

"I thought this was just surveillance," Reid lies.

"Don't be ridiculous."

Reid, of course, is not unaware of the possible fate of their targets—he knows who he's working for—but now in his third year in the Air Force, he is every bit as uncomfortable with what they do as he was when he was first assigned to Creech. He wishes he could ask all the questions. Are there less severe ways to punish Tarek? Will his entire time with the Air Force consist of one hit job after another? Are relationships between officers and enlisted really that terrible? He thinks of his dad, who Reid would pester with a dizzying array of questions when he was a kid. Never once did his dad shunt him away. He answered his every question with infinite patience.

Arjun yawns. "I need coffee," he says.

"I'll get some," Reid says, standing up.

"Make it quick."

On his way to the mess hall, in the dark, he wonders if Tarek's daughter asks questions endlessly, too. He wonders where he'll be assigned after Creech. There's Ramstein in Germany, Kadena in Okinawa, Aviano in Italy. He'd take any of those. What he really wants is something closer to Dayton, close to his dad, though he knows the military will decide his fate for him.

Something squeaks. He stops and pulls out his penlight, shining it into the night. A tiny desert mouse stands on its hind legs in the dirt and peers up at him, nose twitching, sniffing the air.

"Hello, Mr. Mouse," Reid says, quietly. It stares at him curiously. "Or maybe it's Mrs. Mouse. Sorry, I can never tell with your kind."

It ignores his equivocation and quivers its whiskers.

"I'll be on my way. The king needs caffeine," Reid explains, embarrassed for actually feeling apologetic, then snaps off the penlight and keeps walking.

The mess hall is serving Midnight Meals, so he picks up a burrito and a salad for Arjun as well. Back in the cockpit, Arjun inhales the food, and they quietly wrap up the rest of the mission. When they step out of the cockpit, the sky is just beginning to brighten. Reid heads for the shuttle bus back to Las Vegas. Arjun drives. He hasn't once offered Reid a ride back.

"I'll see you later, sir," Reid says.

Arjun grunts, then heads for his car. From the window of the shuttle, Reid watches Arjun's car turn the corner. Before they leave the parking lot, Reid has fallen asleep.

At Fleming's, Emerick sits quietly while Stacey and the sommelier engage in a spirited discussion over tonight's selection. The sommelier gesticulates animatedly when Stacy mentions the vineyards in Piedmont, Italy, she visited three years ago. They exchange their favorite off-the-beaten-path cities in Europe, and they squeal when they discover one in common.

Emerick should be accustomed to this by now—both being ignored and the stodgy conversation—but tonight his lack of sleep is catching up to him. It's true he doesn't know squat about vintage and tannins—he'll drink anything—but he's been unsettled since the start of their dinner when the server spat out, "*tap water?,*" taking Emerick's response and twisting the words into something vulgar. "You'll have the *tap water*?" ("We'll have the sparkling," Stacey interjected, trying to defuse the tension. To Emerick, it felt like she was taking the server's side.)

Emerick's mood sours further when the next server asks how he'd like his steak, and Emerick feels pressured to say "medium rare."

Emerick has been a lifelong medium-well guy, occasionally a well-done. He'd asked Stacey once if this embarrassed her, and after a moment, she said, "Of course not," but he didn't believe her. Ever since, he's ordered his steaks medium rare when dining with her.

Tonight, the server grunts dismissively, as if medium rare is still not rare enough, as if Emerick will always be out of his depth here. Stacey smiles at him encouragingly, but he doesn't smile back.

When they've ordered, Emerick asks Stacey what she's been up to at the university. She launches into a lengthy explanation, using a lot of jargon, and by the time she reaches the part about a potential new opportunity at the law school—greater responsibility, more compensation—he has tuned out. Their Bibb lettuce salads arrive. Emerick bristles a little; it's the server who served the *tap water*. As they eat, Emerick asks Stacey if she's finalized her summer travel plans. An adventurer, Stacey's last two trips took her to Myanmar and New Zealand, where she parasailed, cliff-dove, spelunked, surfed, and rock-climbed. Emerick's only trip in the last five years, which he took a month after Reid left, was to Myrtle Beach, where he fell asleep on the beach every morning and got sunburned.

Stacey lowers her fork. "I've been meaning to ask you."

"Ask me what?"

"Would you like to join me for a week in Monaco this summer?"

"*Monaco*?"

Emerick doesn't know if Monaco is a country or a city, or something else entirely, much less which continent it is on. Whatever and wherever *Monaco* is, Emerick knows the servers there will question the water he orders. He's suspicious of *Monaco* already. Hell. There isn't a city in the world he could afford to travel to. Hell. He can't even afford date night here in Dayton.

Stacey's smile falters, and Emerick wonders if he'd said *Monaco* the way the server spat out *tap water*.

"You don't have to come, of course," she says. "I thought it'd be fun if we traveled together."

"It sounds pricey."

"I'll cover the costs," Stacey says, then shrinks when Emerick's scowl deepens.

It occurs to him that he and Stacey have never once eaten at Applebee's. He knows that he's mentioned, on more than one occasion, how comfortable he feels at a place like Applebee's. He's explained that the restaurant's familiarity is what elevates the passable, if predictable, food into something delicious.

"I don't know," he says. "I've never really considered visiting Monaco."

Stacey looks surprised and disappointed. "What would you rather do?"

Emerick surveys the dining room, the mahogany counters, the endless rows of silverware, the wines in the showcase with their special vintages and expensive tannins ready to be carried out and brandished like trophies. He's convinced the servers in tuxedos gather in the back and wonder out loud what someone like Stacey could possibly see in him.

Emerick lays his salad fork down. "I want to go roller skating."

He doesn't *really* want to roller skate. He cares for skating as much as he cares for Bibb lettuce salad. It's just that Skateworld is cheap, and he can afford to pay, and he knows that if they continue to dine exclusively at Fleming's and if they travel to places like Monaco, he'll one day soon feel compelled to choose how this ends, and he does not want to make that decision.

A year ago, Reid was so distraught at the death of his first surveillance target—the subsequent missile strike killed the man's entire family and their two chocolate Labradors—that Dallas and Mo had rushed to Reid's apartment, armed with pizza and Dallas's PlayStation and terrible jokes, none of which referenced harm to any person or animal. What most upset Reid was that the target was so unsuspecting—how on the surveillance screens, he'd gone about his day like it were any other, how he'd shopped and met with friends and jogged through the city with the certainty of routine and the expectation that he would do it all again tomorrow.

"You watch them day after day and eventually you feel this connection with them," Reid blubbered, and Dallas shushed him and said he didn't have to explain; who *wouldn't* react the way that he had?

"Arjun," Reid answered, and Dallas and Mo had no rejoinder. In fact, earlier that night, Arjun—smug, satisfied—had invited Reid to celebrate the assassination with him and the rest of their unit. Reid told Arjun his stomach hurt.

"Are you guys still together?" Mo asked hesitantly.

Reid shrugged. "He's complicated, but he has his virtues," he said, unsure why he felt so defensive.

"Of course he does," Mo said. Then he added, "Plus he's so hot."

They all looked sad, as if coming to the conclusion that hotness was Arjun's sole virtue. They fell silent, thinking their own thoughts.

Mo said, "We need to get you out of this apartment."

After a minute of brainstorming, Reid asked, "You guys aren't down for bowling, are you?"

Mo and Dallas grinned. They were always down for bowling. They lived in glitzy Las Vegas with its twenty-four-hour neon and never-ending streams of tourists, and they occasionally loved a decadent pool party on the Strip with a celebrity DJ, or a wild night at the Phoenix, but in the end, they'd grown up in small towns, and for them, there would always be inexplicable comfort in returning to things best done away from the big cities, like spending hours at a crumbling bowling alley and snacking on nachos slathered with cheese-equivalent sauce, which at the moment sounded delicious.

Mo stood. "Did you know, young Reid," he said, "that you are talking to the former high school bowling champ of Pleasant Grove, Utah?"

Dallas stood. "Don't worry if you suck," he assured Reid. "I couldn't bowl if my life depended on it."

Reid wanted to thank them, but he wanted to thank them for something much larger than taking him bowling, something beyond their friendship, even. He couldn't quite put it into words, this gratitude swirling in his heart and pushing out the anguish he'd been feeling all night, but based on the way Mo and Dallas were smiling back, he figured they pretty much knew already what it was he wanted to say.

Stacey, it turns out, had been a child prodigy on roller skates, one of Dayton's finest. At Skateworld, under the revolving strobe lights and the pulsing jams of the eighties—still dressed in her Fleming's attire—she captures everyone's attention with her elaborate twirls and pirouettes and, when they bring out the limbo bar, her outstanding limboing, the way she contorts into impossible shapes and slides easily under the bar when it's perilously low.

Emerick soon concedes that he can't keep up. Her speed is too great. Her limbo contortions defy the laws of physics. They can start skating in the same position, but thereafter, the only subsequent times they're together are when she catches up after lapping him, before speeding off once again. When she slows down and joins him, he knows he is holding her back, and Stacey is too competitive—too filled with a passion for speed, for adventure, for something larger than Emerick could ever be—to enjoy skating slowly with him.

So he skates off the rink and leans on the rail and watches Stacey whizz by at her breathtaking speed. In her cashmere blouse and pantsuit and her grimy skates that must be as old as Skateworld itself, Stacey looks as though she has belonged here her whole life. She is beautiful. He retrieves his phone and records Stacey skating. A farewell memento, perhaps. By the next lap, Stacey realizes what Emerick is doing. Each time she returns, she smiles and waves. This time, she leaps and spins, sticking the landing. Cheers and applause erupt. This time, she flails her arms like a windmill, pretending to be out of control. This time, she sticks out her tongue and crosses her eyes. As she passes, her head rotates so her gaze is fixed on Emerick, and he thinks he sees a trace of concern on her face. This time, she looks past the camera at Emerick, smiling this faint smile. This time, she waves at the camera, and she could be saying hello, or goodbye, or I'm still here. This time, she slows and halts before Emerick, and he lowers his phone as she reaches for him.

"Join me?" she murmurs, and Emerick stands there, considering.

His daughter is seven and her name is Sacha, and tonight, Tarek and Sacha are at a carnival that reminds Reid of a cross between an American state fair and a rural amusement park. It is dark, and the night is lit with lightbulbs strung between tall poles. The father and daughter amble from one booth to the next, hands clasped and swinging, undecipherable words streaming from Sacha as she gazes adoringly at her father.

It's early afternoon in Nevada, and outside it is scorching under a cloudless sky, but the cockpit is quiet and dark, save for the glow of the screens and control panel and the dim lights shining from the ceiling. The air conditioners struggle to keep up, and Reid is uncomfortably warm. To his left, Arjun cheerfully steers the drone.

"Guess who got orders?" is how he'd greeted Reid at the start of their shift.

"For when?" Reid had whispered.

Arjun's grin widened. "Soon enough, my friend."

"Tonight?"

Arjun ignored him, leaning forward and whispering into his ear, "I'm going to plow you so hard this weekend, kid, you won't be able to get off the floor," before nonchalantly plopping into his pilot seat.

That was an hour ago. Once again, Reid can't help but cast glances at Arjun's forearms, wide and dense. Today, he finds these arms repulsive. Arjun's sheer physicality is what drew Reid to him in the first place, but the world's axis has shifted.

On the screen, Tarek and Sacha arrive at a glittering carousel, and he helps his daughter climb onto a stallion. Sacha squeals, then leans forward and kisses her father. Tarek's face is so tender that Reid nearly sighs. The carousel rotates, slowly at first. Tarek stands by his daughter's side, gently placing his hand on her back as the carousel quickens and her stallion rises and falls to the cadence of carousel music

Reid can't hear. Sacha grips the brass post, and her gaze is fixed on her father. Reid closes his eyes and fills in the sounds: the calliope music, Sacha's peals of laughter, Tarek's soft words, the distant roar of a roller coaster, the rustle of the breeze.

The drone hovers in a fixed position, invisible high in the sky. Tarek and Sacha disappear around the side of the carousel, then reappear, a smile plastered on Sacha's shining face, Tarek's hand caressing her back.

"Zoom on target." Arjun's voice comes from thousands of miles away.

Reid twists the knobs so hard and Tarek's face enlarges so abruptly that the image becomes pixelated. Then it sharpens, and for the first time, Reid notices Tarek's eyes. They are green and haunting, perfectly set in his narrow, symmetrical face. They are filled with love for his daughter. Filled with longing.

"I said can you hear me." Arjun's distant voice snaps Reid back to the stuffy cockpit.

"What do you want?" Reid's voice is sudden and large and distraught.

Arjun jerks his head in surprise. "What was that, kid?"

"Yes, sir, I can hear you."

Arjun cocks his head, studying Reid. "You all right?"

"Yes, sir." Reid backs off in volume, if not in rancor.

"What's gotten into you?" Arjun barks.

Reid's head is turned away from Arjun. He knows Arjun's surprise will soon morph into rage; he is surprised Arjun isn't angrier already.

A squeak interrupts them, emanating from somewhere in the cockpit between them. They pause and look down. On the control desk, a tiny desert mouse crouches in the space that separates them. The mouse is staring up at the screens, front paws raised, as though surveilling Tarek and Sacha and the whirling carousel. His eyes dart from one screen to another.

"The hell?" Arjun says. "How did it get inside?"

"Why are you doing this, Mr. Mouse?" Reid murmurs.

In the distance, he imagines he hears the breathy notes of the carousel's steam organ, the roar of the roller coaster, the ocean, the wind.

Arjun's hand curls into a fist. His gaze is fixed on the mouse, his forearms are taut, his shoulders tensed. Like a hydraulic press, he raises his fist above the mouse.

Reid faces his boyfriend. "Please, Arjun," he pleads, unable to steady his trembling voice.

"Back down, airman."

It takes both of Reid's hands to cover Arjun's balled fist.

"Let him live," Reid whispers.

GOOD NIGHT, EVERYBODY

"They want me to do it?" Benji repeats, staring at the paddle Emilia tries to shove in his hands. He is dumbfounded; he just never thought anyone would want *him* to do it. For a moment, he's excited to have been noticed by strangers; then embarrassment quickly takes over.

"It's your lederhosen," Emilia explains. "They've been talking about you all night." She points downward. "You can see your junk."

Benji glances down, eyes widening. "Oh no. When did my uniform shrink?"

"It didn't," Emilia points out. "Anyway. His name is David Winkle—they're celebrating his fiftieth birthday. They say they're from Dayton—I think that's in Ohio." She pries Benji's fingers open and wraps them around the paddle, then pats his shoulders and says, "There you go, you ho."

Benji loosens the buckles on his lederhosen. "One question," he says. "How hard exactly do we . . . strike them?"

Emilia nods seriously, as though this is a most appropriate question. "Imagine if you spank him hard enough, you won't ever have to serve frat boys on Friday nights ever again."

Benji puckers his lips. "*That* hard?"

Emilia shakes her head. "Oh no. Much harder. Imagine if you spank him hard enough, then this whole place burns down and we don't have to work here ever again."

Benji gasps. "I had no idea."

Emilia smiles grimly. "Spank the shit out of him, you filthy heat-packing animal."

It's a bustling Sunday night at Hofbräuhaus just off the Las Vegas Strip, and the volume in the cavernous dining hall has climbed to the fevered pitch where people have to yell to be heard. Before Benji got accustomed to the noise, he'd go home every night with dull headaches. Harried servers in black and blue and white lederhosen hoist platters of wiener schnitzels and bouquets of pilsner mugs and carefully navigate between rows of benches. The musicians onstage—they play accordion, zither, and bagpipe—are now taking a break, offering a slight reprieve.

Emilia leads Benji to her section, where a large table is occupied by a group of eight patrons who have clearly been enjoying their libations.

Emilia whispers, "Schoolteachers," to Benji before announcing his arrival with a sweep of her arms.

The matriarch of the group, whose voice is so loud it's like she's speaking into a microphone—Benji heard her all the way from his section—notices him first and springs to her feet.

"That's him! That's him!" she cries. She climbs on top of the table and throws her arms toward the ceiling. "Oh my! Birthday spankings for everybody!"

"Come down, Mabel," one friend pleads.

Benji grips the paddle. In the edge of his vision, Emilia looks more pleased than he's ever seen her. He shoots her a scowl, which widens her smile.

"And where is our birthday boy?" Benji chirps gloomily, brandishing the paddle as if it were a toilet plunger.

David Winkle hops up and makes his way to the head of the table. He bends over and grips the edge of the table.

"You have been a bad boy," Benji recites. He raises the paddle.

"Very bad!" Mabel corrects him. "Terrible! Spank him so hard he can see Chicago from here!"

The other teachers say nothing, subdued by the violence in her comments.

Benji swings and taps David lightly on his buttocks. The drill is two gentle love taps followed by a bone-crushing wallop.

"Yes, yes! Harder!" Mabel cries. She climbs back onto the table.

Benji sighs, then lightly smacks David again, barely making a sound. A displeased murmur arises. They are bloodthirsty, these Ohio schoolteachers. He adjusts his lederhosen and raises the paddle high for the final spank. The schoolteachers have gone bug-eyed. Benji notices a family with two toddler-aged boys at a nearby table. The parents cover the boys' eyes. The boys push at their parents' hands. Benji locks eyes with the mother, who shakes her head at him.

Benji inhales deeply, then winds back and whacks David Winkle so savagely that a sharp crack ricochets across the cavernous room. The paddle has splintered in two. A gasp surges through the restaurant, followed by a stunned silence.

Benji looks down, panting. David Winkle is sprawled out on the ground, face planted on the floor.

"Oh, David Winkle!" Mabel cries. She scrambles off the table, kneels beside him and cradles his head in her lap. "Oh my! Have you died? Did you enjoy it?"

David groans. He struggles to get up. Mabel strokes his head. She leans forward when he cracks open his mouth.

"That," David mumbles, nearly incomprehensible. His eyes are shut. "Was."

"Yes?" Mabel says. "That was what, David Winkle?"

The teachers lean forward with anticipation.

"Magnificent," David moans, then weakly flashes Benji a thumbs-up.

On the stage, the musicians have returned from their break, and the room fills with joyful Bavarian music. Benji raises his broken paddle defiantly, then, feeling stupid, lowers it to his side. He grabs the dessert menu off the table and waves it in the air.

"Who wants apple strudel?" he asks.

Every hand goes up, including David Winkle's.

When Benji arrives back at his apartment that night, his sister, Beverly, is sprawled out on the couch, which means she's already lost everything she made today at her housekeeping job. It infuriates him that companies are allowed to do same-day pay in a city with so many addicts. Benji's only comfort is that he knows his sister would never degenerate to the point of risking her job at the only company still willing to employ her—a small, dingy casino in northeast Las Vegas, where burned-out lightbulbs go unreplaced for months.

Beverly wears only his sweatshirt, and she clutches a bottle of vodka, her grip firm even as she snores lightly. She opens one eye when Benji tries to pry the bottle away.

"Mine," Beverly slurs, struggling to sit up. She tightens her grip. Her breath is so sour that Benji jerks away.

"You should put on more clothes—hey, guess what?" Benji points to the wall behind the couch.

Beverly looks, and Benji snatches the bottle away.

"You used to love this sweatshirt," she says. With surprising dexterity, she snatches the bottle back.

Benji grabs the throw blanket and tosses it to Beverly. "Just cover up."

Beverly unfurls the blanket over her legs and smooths out the wrinkles. She squints. "Did your uniform shrink?"

"I don't want to talk about it."

"Since when have you been this thick?"

"I'm going to bed. You should get your life together."

"You should eat less."

"Whatever. Good night."

"Good night, everybody!" Beverly sings, waving at Benji.

Her taunting words slice through him, but he says nothing and closes his door. He collapses on his bed. He feels powerless and overweight. *Good night, everybody*. If only Beverly knew how much she hurt him with these three words, because he thinks of the last time . . .

. . . it was effortless to follow their dream. Their dream: Beverly's and his. Growing up just outside of Kansas City, they perfected the sibling duo act: Benji on vocals, Beverly on acoustic guitar. They performed for their friends and friends' families and once at their middle school talent show and again during spirit week when they were juniors in high school. Their idols were Donny and Marie Osmond, confirming that they were born with old souls and the Osmonds' destiny was theirs to share. They were exceptional, and they knew it. They just needed luck. Time was on their side. They would watch the *Donny & Marie* show before going to bed, mimicking the way their idols signed off *Good night, everybody*! to rapturous applause.

A year after they graduated, they purchased one-way bus tickets to Las Vegas, because they wanted, more than anything, to become headliners like Donny and Marie. After arriving in Vegas, they took any job they could get: they worked as flyer distributors, served as banquet staff at the Paris casino, and for a short while, dressed up as Olaf and an adorable Minion for tips from intoxicated tourists. Meanwhile, they went to auditions, and though they never made it past the cattle call, they were convinced each time they'd *just* missed the cut and their big shot was just one more audition away. On days off, they practiced their set in their apartment living room, imagining they were performing before thousands in one of the massive venues on the Strip.

Four years later, much has changed. Beverly fell into addiction, slowly at first. It didn't feel crippling, and then suddenly it was too late. They went to fewer auditions, until one day Benji realized that he couldn't recall their last one. Beverly lost her job in accounts payable at a large casino, then her job as a server, then her job as a casino cage cashier, and now she tosses used syringes into heavy-duty trash bags while wearing protective gloves in the casino toilet stalls. After work, she drives home and parks, then walks to the nearest casino, where sympathetic cocktail servers pass her free, watered-down vodka tonics until she's burned through her paycheck on the slot machines. She tells the servers it's just a matter of time before her luck turns around.

As for Benji, Hofbräuhaus was the only place within walking distance that offered him steady hours. He started as a busboy, then became a server when he turned twenty-one. He tolerates his job on some days, and anyway, he needs time to figure out what comes next for the both of them. And though he would never admit this to Beverly, on most days, he hasn't given up on their dream. As long as one of them holds onto this hope, he tells himself, that is enough. But he sure wishes luck would come their way, and soon, because he doesn't know how much more of this he can take.

"They want us to do *what*?" Benji asks.

"They want me to spank the husband while somebody sings happy birthday to him," Emilia says over the din of another busy night, "and since you're the only person in this place who can carry a tune, well . . ."

"Why do we get all the weirdos?"

Emilia, exasperated, exhales. "I don't know, Benji. I just work here. You're asking difficult questions." She grabs her paddle. "Let's get this over with."

She leads him toward Table Three in the far corner, where a middle-aged couple is deep in conversation. As they cross the room, Emilia's scowl morphs into a dazzling smile, and by the time they reach the table, she's transformed into the most enthusiastic server in all of Las Vegas. There is a reason Emilia is six-time Employee of the Month, the repeat winner of discount tickets to Regal Cinemas.

Emilia places her hand on the husband's shoulder and says, "It's your birthday, Derek. You know what that means."

Sonya, the wife, puts down her fork. "He is to be sung to," she says.

"Absolutely," Emilia confirms.

"While being spanked," Sonya adds.

"One hundred percent," Emilia says, brandishing her paddle. Her smile flattens into a stern grimace. "Now if you will assume the position while my colleague serenades you . . ."

Benji realizes that Emilia is doing her best not to burst out in laughter, or maybe in tears.

Derek rises and places his hands on the edge of the table. "Whatever my wife wants," he says. He closes his eyes.

"While my *colleague serenades you* . . ." Emilia says again pointedly.

Benji snaps to attention. He clears his throat. "Happy *birthday* to you . . ." His cheeks redden. He looks down, too ashamed to see if nearby customers are watching. Who is he kidding? Of course they are. Still, he sings, and though he's rusty and this song is stupid, he can't help but think he sounds pretty good.

"Happy birthday *to* you . . ."

Emilia smacks Derek lightly.

"Happy *birthday,* dear Derek . . ."

Emilia smacks Derek a second time.

"Happy birthday to *you.*"

On the final *you,* Emilia wallops Derek, who yelps in surprise. Scattered applause breaks out from nearby tables. Benji doesn't know if they're clapping for Emilia or Derek or him, but in any case, he wants to die.

Derek returns to his seat. "So, I've been disciplined. Now I'll need a scotch, please," he says to Emilia. "To ease the pain."

Emilia disappears, leaving Benji alone at the table.

"You're quite the singer," Sonya says, gazing at Benji. She's been silent this entire time. "Are you a professional?"

This is the first time anybody has called him that. It makes him feel lightheaded.

"I am," he says without thinking.

"I knew it," Derek says. "Can you sing another song? We'll tip, of course."

"I can do the Eagles," Benji says, shyly.

"I love the Eagles!" Sonya exclaims.

Benji launches into "Tequila Sunrise," feeling less self-conscious now. When he finishes, the couple applauds, along with the customers at nearby tables, and this time he knows it's for him. A warm, syrupy elation spreads through his body.

"That was wonderful," Sonya says. "Do you by chance do private parties?"

"Of course," Benji says without thinking.

"We're planning a midnight party next Saturday for our daughter's birthday. She's turning twenty-one," she explains. "We're looking for live music."

"My sister is my partner," Benji excitedly says. "We're really fantastic together."

"Is that so?" Derek says. "Well, we'd love to book you, but here's the thing. We've been having a little trouble finding someone, because the thing is, we live out in . . ."

". . . Pahrump?" Beverly says that night when she gets home from the casino and is ambushed by a frantic Benji speaking at eighty miles an hour. "Benji, that's so far. And the gig is so little."

"This is our *chance,* Bev," Benji cries. "We've been waiting for this our whole lives. How can we turn this down?"

Beverly takes a seat on the couch. She picks up the vodka, then sets it back down.

"I don't know," she says. "So what if the gig goes well? Then what? A backyard in Pahrump isn't going to get us to Caesars Palace. Benji, we're just not good enough."

"Yes, we are," Benji retorted. "I never stopped believing in us. Why else are we even busting our butts here?"

This makes Beverly pause.

“We have to be in Pahrump a little before midnight,” he continues. “We’ll leave here after our shifts, and we’ll be back hours before your next shift.”

“I don’t know,” Beverly says.

Benji sits on the couch beside her. “Come *on*, Bev. Isn’t this what we’ve been preparing for our whole lives? You’ll even have time to hit the slots before we head out there.”

“That’s true,” Beverly admits.

“What do we have to lose?” Benji asks.

On the day of the gig, Benji’s biggest worry is that Beverly might finally hit a winning streak on the slots and abandon him, but to his surprise, she’s already home when he sprints there after his shift. She’s freshly showered and tuning her guitar and humming to herself. She’s wearing makeup for the first time in months, and her hair is sleek and combed. She smiles when he bursts through the door.

“OK, so, fine. I am excited,” she says, and Benji rushes in and embraces her.

He once tried to explain to his parents why he wanted to be famous, how it wasn’t really about the fame—though he wasn’t against that, of course—but about finding a way to communicate with the world around him. Always the reserved one, he nevertheless yearned to connect with people in some meaningful way, and right now, sharing excitement this raw and true with his sister, he’s flooded with gratitude, confident that tonight will draw the two of them closer.

On the car ride over, Benji can’t express how hopeful he is. To his left, Beverly silently steers and focuses on the road before them, her expression inscrutable. He runs through their set, imagining the applause from the crowd, and then he imagines Beverly and him at the Colosseum, performing before a capacity audience of four thousand, and he imagines that one day, they will think back on tonight’s gig in Pahrump, how it all started here.

* * *

They arrive half an hour before midnight and park a few blocks away on a street lined with trucks and vans. When Beverly kills the engine, leaving them in silence, the reality of it all hits them. The streets are abandoned and dark, so much quieter than the Vegas that they know.

"Tell me we're good enough," Beverly says, quietly.

"More than you'll ever realize."

They gather their mic stands and guitar and make their way to Pahrump.

At the front door, Sonya and Derek welcome them, then usher them through the house and to the backyard, where they've set up a large canopy strung with lights. Delicious-smelling smoke wafts from a barbecue grill. Small groups of party attendees are scattered throughout the backyard, creating a lively buzz of conversation. Sonya escorts them to a makeshift stage in the middle of it all. As they set up, she offers them drinks.

"We'll pass, but thank you," Beverly says politely, and that is when Benji knows she is treating this seriously.

Derek introduces them to his daughter, Audrey.

"In seventeen minutes, your entire world is going to open up," Beverly tells her.

Audrey flushes pink. A quiet girl, she thanks Beverly.

At midnight, cheers and party horns and poppers erupt. Derek hands Audrey her first birthday drink—a flute of champagne. Everyone cheers when Audrey downs the champagne and raises the flute. Sonya brings out a sheet cake with white and red frosting, which is quickly divided into little squares and distributed. Derek motions at Benji and Beverly, who have been anxiously waiting for the go-ahead. They jump a little in their chairs. They exchange a panicked stare before Beverly mouths, *we got this*.

Beverly begins by strumming the opening riffs to a Led Zeppelin classic. Benji takes in the crowd that surrounds them, the darkness of the night sky above. He's relieved that it's Beverly who's starting them off and not him. He thinks of the coliseums they will fill in the future. He whispers a prayer into the cool breeze, then begins to sing.

* * *

Two hours later, they wrap up the final song for the night.

Benji is exhausted. He doesn't know how he'd rate their performance. Not terrible, but certainly not amazing, based on the uneven attention from the crowd. In some moments, the crowd was somewhat engaged, applauding and cheering, but in other moments, the crowd paid them no attention, conversing in their groups at an increasingly loud volume.

He glances at Beverly. He can't tell what she's thinking. From her expression, he'd guess she's relieved it's all over. He thinks back and wonders if there were songs he could have sung better. The first two songs, definitely, before he got over his nerves, and several songs toward the end, when the exhaustion set in. Still, if tonight's experience was enough to convince Beverly to resume their auditions, he'll consider it a win.

Derek approaches, his arms embracing the air. He stumbles when he reaches them.

"Wonderful performance, guys," he slurs. His face is flushed, his eyes glazed. "Thank you for coming all the way out here. I'll put your check in the mail first thing in the morning."

"Ohh," Benji and Beverly say in unison, surprised, and then disappointed. Benji thought they'd be paid on the spot because that's how he thought all performers were paid, and he knows Beverly thought so, too.

"OK," Benji says. "Well, I guess we'll be on our way."

"No!" Sonya cries out, joining their circle. "We're bringing out the karaoke machine. You must stay!"

Benji hesitates. Beverly's face is scrunched in concentration.

"Please stay," Audrey slurs, stumbling into the fray. She has drunk too much champagne, and Benji knows she won't last much longer.

"Bev?" Benji says.

Beverly deliberates. Then she asks, "Would you happen to have any vodka?"

* * *

At a little past five in the morning, Benji and Beverly stagger toward their car, stumbling because Beverly is drunk and Benji is so sleepy. Beverly hands her keys to Benji and collapses into the passenger seat, head sinking into her chest. Moments later, she's snoring. The sky is beginning to lighten. A lone blackbird in a nearby tree announces it has awakened.

On the drive back to Vegas, Beverly is slumped down. Benji feels a keen sense of disappointment, in who and what he isn't exactly sure. He suspects it's himself he's disappointed in. Had they nailed the performance, he'd be driving home confident that this was their destiny, of this he is certain. Perhaps he had hoped Derek and Sonya were secretly executives at Caesars Palace and that they'd extend an offer for another gig, as if the birthday party was an audition all along.

He's so tired, but he keeps the radio off so that Bev can sleep. Maybe he'll feel differently tomorrow after a good night's rest. He checks the time. He has ninety minutes to get Beverly home in time for her to get ready for work. He's thankful he doesn't have work today. A jolt of guilt shoots through him; in his fervor, he hadn't considered that when she agreed to the gig, it meant staying awake for two consecutive days. She's still fast asleep in the passenger seat.

He leans forward and squints at the clock on the dashboard. A warning light is on; he doesn't know what it means or how long it's been on. They left Pahrump thirty minutes ago. He can't recall seeing this warning light on the drive up; on the other hand, he wasn't driving then. The road curves, and the steering wheel pushes back slightly. Panic seeps through him. They have a long way to go before they are out of the middle of nowhere.

Benji manages to drive for another ten minutes before the swerving becomes erratic, and he stops the car on the shoulder. When he gets out, he discovers a nail driven into the front right wheel. He stand there and stares at the punctured tire.

"No spare," he hears Beverly say. She has joined him outside.

They squat and examine the tire.

"What do we do?" Benji asks.

The road is mostly deserted. The occasional car roars by; none so much as slow down.

Beverly fishes out her phone. "We gotta get this towed."

"How long will that take?" Benji asks.

They wait an hour before the tow truck arrives. They hitch a ride in the truck, which rumbles at a glacial speed back to Las Vegas. At one point, Benji politely asks if the driver could pick it up just a little. The driver ignores him. By the time they finally drop the car at the garage and make it to their apartment, Beverly is three hours late for her shift. They stumble inside. Beverly sinks into the couch.

"Welp," she says. "I just lost my job."

"Can you tell them you got sick?" Benji asks.

"My boss," she says, "how do I say this—does not believe in days off for any reason."

"Isn't that illegal?"

Beverly laughs. "According to my boss, there's no such thing." She groans. "Whatever. I never liked working there anyway."

It is eleven in the morning. Benji's mind is fried. The past twelve hours have felt like a fever dream.

"Do you think maybe we can start auditioning again?" he asks hesitantly. "We had a couple great moments last night."

Beverly gazes at him furiously. Her hands flail in frustration, but she quickly regains her composure. She steadies her breathing.

"You don't get it, do you?" she says. She checks her watch. "I'm starving. We're getting lunch. Your treat."

Hofbräuhaus has just opened, and the dining room is quiet, with only a few tables occupied. Benji introduces Beverly to Emilia.

"Can you serve me an Erdinger this early?" Beverly asks.

"Girl," Emilia says. "This is a beer hall."

While they wait for their food, Beverly watches a nearby table, where a server is spanking three tourists in Argentina football jerseys—boys who barely look twenty-one—one after another.

"Olé, Olé, Olé!" they cheer each time one of them has been spanked.

"Well," Beverly says, after the tourists sit down and high-five each other. "That was interesting." She puts down her stein and motions for Emilia.

"How much does that cost?" Beverly asks, pointing to another table where a spanking has commenced.

"A spanking?" Emilia says. "Five dollars."

Beverly fishes a crumpled bill from her purse. "Here," she says, pointing at Benji. "My brother needs one."

"I just want to eat and go home," Benji says.

"Shush. Emilia, can you do him the favor?"

"Certainly," Emilia says. She trots off to the kitchen, then returns with her paddle. She motions for Benji to stand.

He reluctantly gets out of his seat, bends over, and places his hands on the edge of the table.

"You've been a bad boy," Emilia chirps, then lightly spanks him, once, twice, then a third forceful time, but Benji is numb; he doesn't feel a thing, not the first or second spank, not the third, not even the pain from the crushing sense of defeat and his realization that maybe—no, *absolutely*—Beverly was right about them all along.

He's getting ready to sit when Beverly stands.

"What the hell was that?" she says. She snatches the paddle. "Let me show you how it's done. Get back into position, Benji. We're not done."

"Bev, please, no."

"I said bend over."

Benji lowers his head once again. Beverly grips the paddle like a seething Catholic nun, her knuckles going white, then whacks Benji so ferociously he cries out.

"Bad boy!" Beverly shrieks, before whacking him again. "Very bad boy! I lost my job because of you!"

"I'm sorry," Benji moans, his buttocks clenched in anguish. "I'm so sorry."

The Argentinian boys observe this beatdown in dismay, all the humor from their own spanking having dissipated. As Beverly continues to pummel him, even Emilia looks on with consternation. The manager steps out from the kitchen, arms crossed, eyebrows furrowed, but he stands at a safe distance. The room has gone silent.

Beverly tightens her grip and spanks him in time with each word: "How! Many! Times! Do! I! Have! To! Tell! You! The! Dream! Is! Over! It's! Over! Over! Over!"

And Benji gets it. He finally understands. He buries his head in his arms. He whispers, "Good night, everybody," quietly, so quietly that nobody could possibly hear him.

SACRAMENT OF CONFESSION

Years ago, in a time before Toby Bekkum, Assistant Pastor at Saint John's Episcopal Church, surrendered his life to Jesus Christ his Lord and Savior—before he took up his cross and chose a life of penance and prayer—he was quite the skank ho who could not get enough admiration from women. Man-Bacon Bekkum, his fraternity brothers called him, and he'd finesse pomade through his powerful curly hair before they strutted to the college rec to shoot hoops and admire their jawlines in the locker room mirrors. Weekends consisted of socials with sparkly sorority sisters, and a saunter through campus between classes meant frequent stops to chat with friends passing by, and generally speaking, life was really vigorous and amazing.

Toby scratches his thinning hair and thinks about the heathen, unencumbered life he once enjoyed, and while he can't definitively say he wishes he could go back, he recalls these days with wistfulness and nostalgia. He is thirty-eight years old, and his body is grinding down. He's increasingly aware of the extra beat it takes him to rise from bed every morning, of the extended rest he needs after a workout, how conducting back-to-back sermons leaves him feeling sore the following day.

Anyway, he is reminded of this because his penitent—seventy-six-year-old Mabel Rogerson, his first-grade teacher at Southeast Dayton Phase Two Elementary School—has been in the confession booth for the last twenty minutes and is confessing the hell out of her transgressions from when she was in college. Toby can't recall the last time he saw Mabel at church, and though he would never consider trying to rush her out of confession, he wonders why she chose today of all days to spill these secrets. His attention is drifting, his patience wearing thin.

"And *then* after Herbert came *Clyde*," Mabel continues. "Now Clyde was a real Gentleman, and his butt was like a cement truck—oh my! Lord forgive me I am getting hot and bothered!"

Through the veiled lattice, Toby hears Mabel smack her lips.

"Let's stick with the confessions," Toby says absentmindedly.

It's a sweltering Monday afternoon—Dayton is in the midst of yet another summer heat wave—and he's hungry and tired.

There's a rap on the far end of the booth.

"Hey, are you done yet?" a young man's muffled voice calls out. "There's a pretty long line out here."

"Wait your turn, Eric Wagner," Mabel snaps. "I'm very busy."

"Crap. Sorry, I didn't know it was you, Mrs. Rogerson."

"Now, where was I?" Mabel asks Toby.

"Clyde and his rock-hard butt."

"Oh yes!" Mabel cries, clapping. "This is so exciting!"

"Actually, I'm not sure you've been told correctly what's supposed to happen in a confes—"

"Romping with Clyde at the swimming pool was the *best*. With him, I *never* felt alone!"

"Let's go to the part where I absolve you of your sins," Toby says. "Now these are things you did a long time ago, so actually you're good. You're forgiven. You can go." Toby checks his watch.

"Well, I wasn't quite done," Mabel says. "After *Clyde* there was—"

"Totally forgiven. You may go in peace."

"How about you, Toby?" Mabel presses her face to the veil. "Don't you ever want to share your feelings?" she says. "Communication is a two-way street, you know."

"That's not how this works and also we really shouldn't be addressing each other by name during—"

"Hogwash," Mabel says. "I've known you since you wore diapers. You can share anything with me." Mabel draws open the veil as if it were a window curtain and peers at him through the lattice. Upon making eye contact, she waves enthusiastically.

"Oh my god, you can't do that," Toby exclaims, sliding the veil shut. "Mrs. Rogerson, please. You're stressing me out."

Mabel draws it open again. "Tell me your darkest, freakiest secrets. Didn't they call you Man-Bacon back in the day?"

"What? *No.*" Toby slides the veil shut.

Mabel draws it open. "Don't lie to me, Dad Bekkum. Go on, now."

"It's Father . . . Bekkum." He sighs. He will not be leaving anytime soon, not at this rate. He cares for his congregation, and on most days, he tolerates the job—enjoys it, even. But sometimes he just wants to go home and lock the bedroom door and shut out the world.

And this is what he does that night. Alone in his apartment—Marta is working her second job, though he doesn't want to think about that—he scarfs down his microwaved rigatoni, retreats into the second bedroom, and boots up his deteriorating laptop. Toby's dark, freaky secret that he'll confess to nobody—not Mabel, not God, certainly not Marta, not that she is around much—is his obsession with twenty-one-year-old Hermione Herro, future internet sensation. With a can of ginger ale by his side, he opens her live stream. There she is in her wizarding robe, holding her wand and wearing a bright purple wig. Her makeup is thick and creamy, her glasses large. There are six other viewers. Hermione Herro leans forward in her gaming chair and waves.

"Bacon Boy!" she exclaims. "Welcome! Herro! I missed you! How was your day?" She lifts her wand and casts a magical spell on Toby.

The stress from his day is evaporating already. Is he ashamed? Of course he is. Will he do the right thing and stop watching her streams? Well, let's not go crazy. He recently subscribed to her channel for an additional twenty-four months; he'll reassess when his subscription expires.

"Well, *my* day was *magical,*" Hermione continues. "We were discussing Gym Hero's girlfriend problems."

In the chat box, Gym Hero types a sad face.

"Why are we talking about him again," Toby mutters. He's gathered that Gym Hero recently graduated from high school somewhere in the Northeast and has somehow convinced Hermione Herro that he's more handsome than Toby suspects he is.

"Now you listen to me, Gym Hero," Hermione says sternly, waving her wand at the screen. "You are attractive, athletic, and compassionate, and you deserve to be with somebody who appreciates you."

Gym Hero fills the chat box with an array of hand-heart emojis.

"This little shit," Toby grouses.

Have I ever mentioned I was the captain of my wrestling team? Toby types, unable to stop himself.

Hermione claps her hands. "That is *wonderful,* Bacon Boy!" she exclaims. "I *knew* you were an athlete!"

Was that the girls' wrestling team? Gym Hero types.

Toby fumes, but he is terribly slow with comebacks, so instead he takes a defiant sip of his ginger ale.

"Now Gym Hero, let's stay away from jokes of that nature," Hermione admonishes him, her face clouded with disappointment. "Oh no. We lost two viewers. Can you please stop fighting? We should all get along."

Fine, Gym Hero types.

Fine, Toby types.

From beneath her desk Hermione retrieves her ukulele and strums beautiful, harmonious chords.

"La la la," she sings. "Somewhere over the rainbow, way up high, and the dreams that you dreamed of, once in a lullaby."

Toby is mesmerized.

My first-grade teacher confessed today—he types before deleting and starting over. My grandmother told me today about her sex life when she was young, and it made me uncomfortable.

"I understand," Hermione says melodically as she strums. "It's weird to imagine old people being sexually active, especially when we look up to them. Even when they're talking about their younger selves. Just remember, one day you and I will be old, if we're lucky, and we'll be reflecting on our younger selves, too."

Toby pictures himself in his twilight years. Will he still be suffering through endless confessions and delivering sermons to inattentive congregations? Will he still be venting to some broke college-student streamer who knows nothing about him? He reaches for his wallet. He wonders if he has made a terrible mistake, committing his life to the church. Hermione Herro puts down her ukulele and covers her mouth.

"Oh my *god*, Bacon Boy," she gasps. "Thank you *so* much for the five-hundred-dollar donation."

Toby types a heart emoji.

"Thanks for listening," he says quietly.

For a moment, guilt and shame overtake him. Then he closes the tab and deletes his browsing history.

Toby wakes the next morning and stumbles into the kitchen to find Marta in her flight attendant uniform, leaning on the counter and cradling a coffee cup. A packed sports bag lies by her side. He doesn't disclose what he knows; he doesn't casually ask about the bikini and the platform heels stuffed in the bag, or ask how much she was tipped last night grinding on the laps of groomsmen and divorcés and fraternity brothers celebrating twenty-first birthdays. At any rate, he doesn't want to hear details. Mostly, he wants to know how she manages with so little sleep—he vaguely recalls her slipping into bed sometime early this morning, and he's thankful that she still sleeps in the same bed as him—but instead he forces a smile and cheerfully greets her. Outside the kitchen window it is dark and gloomy. It has begun to rain.

Marta lifts her cup. "I'm going out with my girlfriends after work," she says, and the ease with which she lies never fails to sting.

In her day job, she works the flight from Dayton to Chicago and three hours later the flight back. He imagines her between flights at the terminal's sports bar, laughing with her fellow crew members as passengers stream by. And he imagines her later that night onstage, topless and gyrating before a roomful of pitiful men. *Why won't you just tell me?* he wants to ask. But he knows she's likely ashamed of her double life, so he mumbles, "Drive safe," then awkwardly waves goodbye as she leaves.

And then it's just him in the apartment. He wishes he could dash outside and wave Marta down and, when she rolls down the window, say, *Let's talk. Please. We used to share everything.* But then she'd say, *Fine, what is it you want to discuss?* And he wouldn't be able to put into words what he wants to say. No, what he'd prefer is for her to turn back and burst through the apartment door and say, *I miss you, I miss our talks, let's fix things,* and he'd casually agree, as if he hadn't given it much thought, though his heart would thump furiously, and he would summon all his willpower to refrain from breaking down and telling her how alone he's felt since they drifted apart.

In the back room of the church, Toby leads Narcotics Anonymous. Joanne shares with the group her distress over catching sight of the scars on her teenage son Teddy's forearms from years of crystal meth injections. Carrie doesn't know how much longer she can bear her husband skipping dinner to watch porn in the basement. Bert Reyes's father is addicted to beating Bert's mother. There's a nervous energy and a sense of aggression in the air, and Toby fears he won't be able to keep things from spiraling out of control in these final minutes.

"Why would Teddy do this to me?" Joanne, the worried mother, sobs.

"I understand," Toby says soothingly.

"How could you?" she snaps. "You've never had kids."

"Come on, now," Carrie says, putting a hand on Joanne's shoulder. "We're all hurting."

Joanne sniffs. "Your problems are nothing compared to mine," she says.

Carrie pulls back her arm and scooches her folding chair away.

Joanne's sobs intensify. "You hate me. Just like my son does."

"I hate my dad," Bert shares, staring at the ceiling.

"Now, Joanne," Toby says. "Nobody hates you. This is a good time to remember that our Lord loves us all."

"The Lord will destroy him," Bert sings. "Meaning my dad," he explains. He tilts his head up at the ceiling again. "Joanne's kid, too," he adds, "if the crystal meth doesn't first."

Joanne bawls.

"Stop that, Bert," Toby warns him. "And Carrie, Jesus loves your husband, too, despite his porn addiction. We will help you get through this."

"Actually," Carrie says, "sometimes I enjoy watching a little porn myse—"

"The Lord will destroy *you*," Bert sings, thrusting his fingers at Carrie.

"Stop! Everybody!" Toby yells. He jumps up, knocking his folding chair over. "Guys. Come on. What's gotten into us? We are here to receive *and* offer support. Now if we can think back to Deuteronomy and recall that our Lord will never leave us—"

"I'm leaving my husband," Carrie announces. "There. I said it. I'm getting a divorce. I am. I've decided."

"Over a little *porn*?" Toby asks, amazed.

"It's a *lot* porn, Toby," Carrie says crossly. "And why should I have to suffer through this? I can find someone who will treat me with respect." She sits up in her chair and squares her shoulders.

Bert and Joanne study her figure and nod.

Carrie stands. "I feel much better. Thank you, Pastor Bekkum." She faces Joanne and Bert. "Best of luck, you guys. You have my solidarity. But you should consider taking matters into your own hands." She spins and exits the room.

"He should've kept his browser on private mode," Bert sings.

Joanne stands. "I'm telling Teddy he needs to stop the drugs or else I'm kicking him out," she says tearfully.

"I'll be here for him," Toby tells her. "But he also needs a doctor."

And then it's just Toby and Bert.

"Soo," Bert says. He scooches his chair toward Toby.

"So," Toby says, scooching his chair away.

"I think I'll stay here for a while," Bert announces.

"Why?"

Bert pulls up his sleeve, revealing a mosaic of bruises, scars, and what look like burn marks. Toby swallows hard.

"Your dad beats you, too?"

"I told him he needs to stop spying on my mom in public, but I picked the wrong time to tell him."

"You need to get out of there. Surely there's a place you can go."

"There is," Bert says. "There's plenty of places."

"Then why would—" Toby's voice trails off.

"My mom needs me. She won't leave." He shrugs. "Anyway. I'm sure you grew up with normal parents."

"I did," Toby admits.

They are slumped in their folding chairs, avoiding each other's gaze and lost in their thoughts. A bleak silence settles in the room. The yelling from minutes ago feels to Toby as if it occurred days ago. He's had a blessed life, he knows that. Life isn't meant to be perfect. And he's ashamed that it takes speaking with someone like Bert to remind him of this.

"Can I hang out here for a bit?" Bert says, breaking the silence. "Before I go back to that hellhole?"

"As long as you'd like."

Hours later, after Bert has left, Toby drives five blocks from the church to Dayton Mystique. In the parking lot, he dons his Bengals cap and sunglasses, and steps out of the car. Inside, the music is deafening and there are vast clouds of cigarette smoke. When he was a college student, the place filled him with vigor and a sense of wonder; now, it reeks of despair and surrender. On the stage, a woman even older than Toby tiredly spins on a pole. He slides into a chair at an empty table in the corner, lowers the bill of his cap, orders a ginger ale, and scans the stage.

He spots Marta at the far end of the room. She is speaking earnestly with a man dressed in a suit. The man is significantly younger than Toby and, based on the man's attire and posture, considerably wealthier, too. It's just the two of them, and she's doing most of the talking. Even from here, Toby can see the man is good-looking. A woman approaches Toby's table.

"Hey, sexy," she says. "Why don't you come closer to the stage?"

He ignores her, and her smile fades. When she realizes he isn't going to speak, she shrugs and walks away.

Toby is studying Marta. He tries to make out her words, but it's dark, especially with his sunglasses. It bothers him that they aren't doing anything physical; they are simply talking, like he and Marta used to, and in a way that suggests they are actually interested in what the other is saying. The server brings Marta a cocktail and the man what looks like a scotch. They gesture at the server, and she joins them. The three engage in a lively conversation, smiling and laughing. Gloom overtakes Toby, and he's relieved when Marta's boss approaches their table and taps his wife on the shoulder. Before she stands and follows her boss to the stage, she places a hand on the man's shoulder. He leans forward and gestures at her encouragingly.

Toby gets up and exits the club and sits in his car, where he stews. It's Marta's decision how to live her life, he reminds himself. He feels inadequate, helpless. Just once, four months ago, Toby gathered the courage to confront her, if only obliquely.

"I feel like I'm no longer satisfying you," he'd said.

They were in the apartment, eating dinner together, a rarity.

"That's a fair assessment," Marta agreed, chewing her penne.

Toby was afraid to ask what specifically made him bad in bed. Was it the weight he'd put on? Was it his hygiene? Was he selfish? He dreaded the possibility of that last one. He wondered if he'd become oblivious in his advancing age. He averted his gaze, and when she realized he'd dropped the subject, she returned to her taciturn self.

Toby sits in his car in the parking lot. Maybe she keeps her secrets so she won't hurt his feelings. This idea, more than anything else, wounds him so deeply that he covers his face and moans.

I had a rough day, Toby types later that night.

"Oh no, Bacon Boy," Hermione Herro exclaims, her purple wig reflecting the light from her desk lamp. "Tell me *everything*."

Hermione's viewership is growing—there are thirty-seven viewers—and Toby is excited for her and also annoyed to have to compete for her attention.

I think my wife is going to divorce—he begins to type, then starts over. I think my girlfriend isn't interested in me anymore.

He's lying about having a girlfriend, Gym Hero types.

"You be nice, Gym Hero," Hermione admonishes him. "Right now we're going to help Bacon Boy work through this." She picks at her ukulele. "Now tell me. How long have you guys been together?"

Seventeen years.

Hermione's eyes widen. "Seventeen years? How old are you?"

Toby swears. Seventeen months. Sorry typo.

"Seventeen months is a long time to be with somebody," Hermione says. "A lot can happen. What kinds of discoveries have you made about each other in that time?"

That my wife's a stripper, he thinks.

I might have become a boring person, he types instead.

You definitely did, Gym Hero types.

"Oh, Bacon Boy," Hermione exclaims. "You are most certainly not boring. You are young and exciting and full of surprises!"

Toby resists the urge to reach for his wallet.

"And then again," Hermione continues, "some relationships just run their course, and sometimes it takes both parties to realize this, in which case it's best to go your separate ways in a way that doesn't undermine your future relationships."

Toby's face falls.

Gym Hero pastes a website link into the chat box. Against his better judgment, Toby clicks on the link and is led to a website selling blowup dolls.

"Motherfucker." Toby grits his teeth.

"Stop that, Gym Hero," Hermione says. She twirls her wand at the screen. "Bacon Boy, I am casting a spell on you for everything to work out exactly how things were meant to be." She flicks her wand, then switches to her ukulele.

"La la la," she sings. "There is a house way down in New Orleans they call the Rising Sun, and it's been the ruin of many a poor boy, and God I know I'm one."

With growing dismay, Toby watches Hermione's viewer count tick up, now at forty-five.

"You are loved, Hermione," he whispers, before logging out for the night and scrubbing his history.

The next morning, Toby is brewing a pot of coffee when Marta enters the kitchen, her hair damp from the shower.

"Coffee's almost ready," he says.

The machine sputters, and Toby hands her a mug. He steadies his breathing. It's now or never.

"Are you seeing somebody else?" he asks.

Marta stares at him in silence, her expression inscrutable, then asks, "What do you think?"

"I think yes, you are."

Marta crosses her arms. "I have an idea," she says tiredly. "Why don't you find out from your online sorceress friend? What is her name?

Bellatrix? Gandalf? Aren't you paying her enormous fees for all the answers? By the way, where are you getting all that money?"

Toby's mouth drops open.

Marta walks to the sink and pours out her coffee.

"Do you ever wonder," she continues, "what it's like being the wife of a pastor?"

He's silent. He has never wondered this.

"It's not easy," she says. "For starters, nobody will share anything with me, as if the first thing I would do is tell you everything. Also, nobody wants me as a friend. They're convinced I would spend all my time judging them or praying for them." She's at the door now. "I'm not seeing anybody else. I've never cheated on you. I'd divorce you first." She steps outside and shuts the door. Then she reopens it, sticking her head inside. "If you're serious about fixing things between us," she says, "you need to stop all communication with your online witch friend." She waits for his reaction, and when he doesn't speak, she says, "I thought so," and then she closes the door.

"Bless me, for I have sinned."

The boy is young, still in his teens. On his bench, Toby feels stiff and old and tired.

"Go on, then," Toby prods him.

The boy speaks haltingly. "I guess what's on my mind is I'm not sure I believe in God anymore. I'm thinking about taking a break from all of this."

"Attaboy," Toby whispers.

"Excuse me, Father?"

"I meant please continue," Toby says. "Why is it that you feel this way?"

"I'm just not sure this religion thing is worth the effort. I don't know. It's so confusing."

"Hell yeah," Toby says, even more quietly.

"Father, are you OK?"

"Well, your sense of hearing seems to be just fine. Look. If you feel the need to take a break, take the break. We'll be here when you return. These things get harder the older you get. Now's the time to do it."

"Oh wow, really? It's that easy? This is awesome. Thank you, Father."

The bench creaks as the boy stands.

"Well, have a good day, Father." And then it is silent.

When Toby exits the confession booth, he bumps into a furious Father O'Connell.

"Oh God, you scared me," Toby says.

"What the hell was that?" O'Connell demands.

"What was what?"

"What you just told that kid." His face tightens. "How in the world does that come close to adhering to the Sacrament of Confession?"

Toby is silent. He has never seen the man this upset.

"Also," O'Connell says, "we should talk about how you've been stealing from the tithes and doing God-knows-what with the money."

Toby freezes, forgetting to breathe for a moment. Then he inhales deeply. He avoids O'Connell's gaze and focuses on the wall, where a crucified wooden Jesus frowns, also disappointed in him.

O'Connell sighs. "Look, Toby. Perhaps it's a good idea if you take some time off. Ask yourself if this is really what you want. Ministry, like marriage, is a lifelong commitment."

Toby's sense of shame deepens. "Where would I go?"

"Wherever you need to." O'Connell clasps Toby's shoulders. "You're not a bad guy. It breaks my heart knowing we don't pay you enough. Now go. Get ahold of yourself. Come back with a renewed vigor for what we do. Figure out a way to support yourself without stealing."

"What should I do?" Toby asks as O'Connell walks away.

"What we always do, my grim preacher," O'Connell says over his shoulder. "We confess."

"I'm not a grim preacher," Toby calls out, but O'Connell is gone.

* * *

Tonight there are 173 viewers, many of whom are pouring their life's troubles into the chat and seeking Hermione's counsel, mostly about relationship troubles but also family problems, fights with friends, stress at school. One viewer recently lost his cat and his will to live.

"Guys," Hermione says, her voice quavering, the stress lines on her face visible on the screen. "I can't keep up with your requests. If you can just slow things down, then I will get to you all eventually."

This only speeds up the pace, and the messages in the chat box flow even more furiously. Hermione wrings her hands.

"Guys, please," she pleads, and, rubbing her temples, she accidentally knocks off her purple wig, revealing severe alopecia and strands of hair that sprout from her otherwise bald head like stringy reeds. The shape of her head resembles the end of a potato.

The flow of messages stops.

Toby gasps. He had no idea. The wig, the glasses, the visual distractions placed carefully throughout her dorm room. Now it all makes sense. He quickly recovers. He was caught by surprise, that's all, and in the crucial moments that follow, his fondness for Hermione rushes back. He doesn't doubt her kindness, nor her gift of raising others up in their time of need.

The other viewers do not feel the same. The chat box fills with a litany of *WTF* and *The hell is this* and *Bro you're a catfish*.

Hermione fits the wig back onto her oddly shaped head, looking shocked and embarrassed. "Oh gosh, I'm so sorry," she squeaks. She stares into her screen.

Toby knows that she is watching her viewer count. The number in the corner keeps dropping: ninety-seven, seventy-one, fifty-eight, twenty-three.

Hermione slumps in her seat. "Oh gosh," she warbles. Her hands flail, taking on a frantic life of their own. "Oh gosh," she cries.

You cappin' ho, a viewer writes in the chat box, and her viewer count drops to eleven.

Hermione throws her hands in the air. "So is this it?" she says, her voice hollow. "Am I done for?"

Don't give up, Toby writes. You'll get through this. You'll rebuild.

He swallows hard. No one should be alone when they most need somebody.

We with you, Hermione, Gym Hero chimes in. We here for the magic. That's what we care about.

Hermione's crying now. "You guys," she whispers, removing her wig.

WTF put that shit back on, somebody types. Hermione tearfully mouths an apology, adjusting her wig.

I have to go, Toby types. He lingers for a moment, whispers a prayer, then pushes the unsubscribe button. His screen goes dark.

"I'm so sorry," he says quietly.

He sits in the back, hidden in the dark. Mystique is mostly deserted; a few men are sprawled on chairs in the front, and others are scattered at different tables, alone. Marta dances by herself. From Toby's vantage, she's dwarfed by the expanse of the stage. Pulsing strobe lights on the ceiling and fog rising from machines at the foot of the stage cast her silhouette in a misty blue. Through the speakers, a glam rocker pines over her former lover to the hollow beat of a drum. The men in the audience gaze up at Marta, then lower their eyes and return to their drinks. Toby wonders if they have partners at home, or families, friends at least. He wonders if the life of a flight attendant is not as glamorous as he has imagined.

It was loneliness, he knows, that drew him to ministry, a loneliness that started in college, even as he was surrounded by his fraternity brothers, and then never went away. He imagines Hermione staring into her own future, so bleak and bald and devoid of magic. If God really created humans for the purpose of sharing love, then why did God make him so stunningly bad at this? It's this, more than anything, that convinces him he is not fit to serve.

Fog envelops Marta as she spins on the pole and tilts her head toward the ceiling. The rocker laments her unrecoverable past. The bassline traverses the floor, makes its way to the back of the room, tingling

Toby's feet. A chasm separates Marta from her onlookers. She leans away from the pole and raises her arm, as if in prayer. He imagines her pointing at a sky filled with single-seat planes that crisscross the horizon. She gazes out into the audience. Toby can hardly breathe. She is beautiful.

PAPER CRANES

You wouldn't recognize me standing there looking this confident. I'm the obstacle to everybody trying to get into the club. They want to roll their eyes at my snug shirt, at the blue ink that snakes out my sleeve, and they're wary of me, scared, maybe, but whatever, they just want to get past.

I work the door at a nightclub in Roppongi from evening until early morning. Sometimes I go inside and break up fights, and sometimes I throw out drunk Navy kids. In the morning, I get paid in cash and take the train back to Kamisoshigaya, and then I'm supposed to go to class, but they don't take attendance for us study abroad students.

The other students in the program take the coursework very seriously. They huddle in the lounge and argue over kanji and conjugation. They greet each other in Japanese and practice bowing. They don't look up when I pass. I'll run into them in the morning when I return with pit stains on my shirt and bloodshot eyes and forearms caked in cigarette ash. Sometimes they'll greet me cautiously. In any case, we don't talk much.

The only one I get along with is my roommate, Jason, from Madison. He has the disposition of a golden retriever. He tells me he wishes I'd smile more.

"Be happy, Andrew," he says. "We're in Japan!"

"I am happy," I tell him. "I just don't show it."

He sings, "If you're happy and you know it—"

"Shut the fuck up."

Where I come from, smiling can get your ass beaten: Miami Chapel in west Dayton, the most defeated part of a city that's been prostrate for who knows how long. To come of age in Miami Chapel is to accept there's no getting out.

For the bouncer job interview, I slid between two middle-aged managers who acted drunk and pretended they were about to throw fists.

"No," I said.

"Very good," one manager declared, satisfied.

"What would you do if four men wanted entry?" asked the other.

"That depends on how much they're willing to spend."

"Do you always look this angry?" asked the first one.

"I'm not angry."

They asked if I could start that night. I could. I desperately needed the money. I had to be the brokest student ever to study abroad.

I was the brokest person you knew.

Coming from where we do, that's saying something. You: our sixth-grade teacher, toughest teacher ever. You called us out when we slacked off on our homework. We saw you on the streets one day holding hands with Mrs. Jacobs, who would years later be our English teacher. We approached you while acting like the shithead seventh grade gangsters we thought we were, and Mrs. Jacobs quickly stepped away from you. I was taller than you by then.

I said, "You're a badass teacher, Mrs. Matsumoto. Maybe one day I can find love like you did with Mrs. Jacobs."

And Mrs. Jacobs cried, and you coughed, insisting you had a dry throat, and you and Mrs. Jacobs invited us for pizza down the street, and we said yes because we never turned down food.

* * *

When I wake up late that afternoon, light streams through the paper window screens. The others aren't back from campus. The hallway is silent. I've never enjoyed waking up feeling alone. I walk to the kitchen in my boxers and peer into the fridge. It's stuffed with beer and fried pork. I fill a glass with water from the faucet. After working all night, I try to keep it clean when I can.

The others, talking excitedly, soon file in through the front door. Their faces fall when they see me standing there half-naked.

"Carry on," I say. I lean on the wall and take a swig of water.

They squeeze by me, staring ahead. Jason's last. He fist-bumps me.

"We want to go to your club tonight. Can you let us in?"

A quarter of the students are teenagers.

"No."

He blinks.

"Just kidding," I say.

He grins. This will be his first time at a nightclub. "Should I dress up?" he says. "What should I wear?"

"This is Tokyo. Wear a t-shirt."

"I was thinking slightly formal. Should I go shopping?"

"No."

He checks his watch. "I have time to go shopping if I leave now. I'll see you tonight, OK?"

That night, the club's packed when three local women—two in their early twenties, the third in her late thirties—approach and then stare me down. They start with my face, then trace the contour of my neck and chest and stop at my crotch. Being white in Japan is interesting because for a country that emphatically discourages staring, they sure don't apply the same rules with me.

I wait for them to look up. They're intoxicated, no doubt, but not to the point where I have to deny entry. They fire off crude jokes, unaware that I can understand them, then giggle at their brazenness. I take it back. Only the two younger women give me their attention. The third stands there looking sober and bored. She's dressed like her friends in a crop top and midi skirt, but everything else about her says she isn't feeling it tonight, probably because her friends are comically thin and confident, and I can tell they consider themselves superior to her. I want to tell her going in will only make her more miserable. As I wave them through, she walks in last and meets my gaze and smiles this tired smile that raises the hairs on my arms, and then she steps inside and is gone. Dazed, I stare at the spot where she just stood.

Then Jason hollers from down the street, "Watch out! Party people coming through! Slay!"

He leads a parade of students to the door and greets me like a long-lost friend. The other students, keeping a distance, stand around and fiddle with their phones.

He shows off his new shirt, a sparkly turquoise button-down that has no business existing in this decade.

"How do I look?" he asks. He can't contain his excitement.

"That shirt's something."

"I know! I'll keep you posted on everything that happens inside," he tells me.

The other students file inside without saying anything to me. As Jason enters, he turns around and flashes me a thumbs-up.

The next few hours are a blur. Three tough white guys from the Navy base play nice, knowing their odds.

"Badass tat, bro," one says, and all three pull back their sleeves to reveal tribal bands.

"Where you from, bro?" another asks eagerly.

I shut this down and wave them in, and they scurry inside before I change my mind. A boy and a girl leave in each other's arms and stumble down the street. They are faking it. Neither is close to being intoxicated. A minor celebrity I recognize from the movies heads inside along with her handlers, but not before she cops a feel of my arm and claps and squeals. A second later, the paparazzi catch up. I have standing orders to let through specific ones, and I wave those in.

Just as I'm getting sleepy, my colleague emerges and takes my position for the next thirty minutes. I cross the street and get a coffee from a café and sit by the windows. Groups of partiers rambunctiously storm past while zombified salarymen, their suits wrinkled and frayed, shuffle back to their studio apartments; a street performer taps her guitar fretboard and quietly sings a years-old Green Day hit. All these strange souls of the night yearning for connection. I sip the hot coffee and watch the performer. You would have yelled at her to loosen up and sing with abandon. Then you would have opened your purse and dumped all your cash into her guitar case.

You discovered my parents had skipped town when I was seventeen. You found out when you rapped on the window of the van they left me. You said loud enough for everybody in the Walmart parking lot to hear, "Andrew, we literally just looked at each other. Stop pretending you're asleep."

And when I rolled down the window, you saw all my stuff in the back seat, and you covered your mouth with your hands.

Twenty minutes later I was stuffing my face at Burger King while you and Mrs. Jacobs, in hushed, urgent voices, struggled to come up with a plan.

"Are you able to pay for food? How are you affording it?" Mrs. Jacobs asked me, her voice quivering.

"Isn't that obvious?" you snapped. "Andrew is a survivor if I've ever seen one." You turned to me. "Are you able to pay for food? How are you affording it?"

"I have jobs," I mumbled.

One job was as an overnight stocker at Walmart, where they let slide the squatted parking spot. Your shoulders stiffened. You coughed into your clenched fist.

"He needs somebody to check on him every night," Mrs. Jacobs said.

You said, "We're taking our walks through the Walmart parking lot from now on." You turned to me. "Did you hear that? We're bringing you dinner every night, so don't go causing trouble." You coughed again.

You told me I needed to get as far away from there as I could.

"Dayton," you spat, your face tight with frustration. "God has abandoned this shit-stain of a city. But don't you worry. You'll be seeing so much of me you'll get tired of my face."

"Actually, I already feel that—"

"You shut up, Andrew."

In the café, I pick at the square paper on my table advertising the izakaya down the street. I fold it as I continue to watch the revelers amble by. Moments later, I'm holding an origami paper crane. I can read the Japanese writing—*10% off all drinks!*—on its crease.

I am being watched. I look up. It's the woman from before, the sober one. The hairs on my arms rise again.

She points at the crane. "Where did you learn to do that?" she asks in English.

"It's a long story."

She sits in the seat beside me. "My friends deserted me."

"Then they're not your friends."

"Serves me right for coming," she says.

"Why did you?"

She reaches into her purse, pulls out a wedding band, and places it back onto her finger. "My husband has gone out again—he says with his friends. But he won't come back until tomorrow, and after so many times, you start wondering."

I wonder how it must feel to be so lonely that you're willing to put up with being ignored by friends who aren't really your friends.

"Why don't you leave?" I say.

"My husband or my friends?"

"Oh."

She stands. "I'm Kumiko," she says. "I'll wait for you to finish your shift."

I watch as she crosses the street and disappears into the club.

* * *

You were the toughest teacher and the toughest person I've ever known. I never saw you cry, though once you came close. I finished my shift at one of my jobs—the one you helped me get at the library, where I put away books and DVDs—and I was on my way back to my van when five kids jumped me. They took everything I had. But the joke was on them. All that effort for three dollars and a library card.

An hour later, you and Mrs. Jacobs banged on my window until I roused from my stupor. You were armed with one of those blue cookie tins that people put their sewing things in, except yours was filled with hydrogen peroxide and gauze and cotton swabs. My eyes were swollen, and my lip trickled blood, and I was dizzy and reeling.

Mrs. Jacobs pleaded, "Will you stop being so stubborn and move into our spare bedroom already?"

I was about to mumble, "I already told you, I don't want to hear you and Mrs. Matsumoto go at it every night," but you said, "You zip it, Andrew," and you got to work dabbing the hydrogen peroxide on my cuts, which stung like a motherfucker, but I had to admit it felt good not being alone in the van.

You got me patched up, and maybe you sensed I was tired, because you placed my head on your lap. Your body was trembling. You'd developed a steady cough by then, and your body was this force of warmth and tremors and periodic convulsions. I rested my eyes.

"If you guys have to go, I'll understand," I said, trying to sound nonchalant.

"We're not going anywhere," you said flatly.

Eventually, my exhaustion took over, and I fell asleep for I'm not sure how long. When I woke up, disoriented and a little panicky, it was just getting dark, and you and Mrs. Jacobs were there by my side, talking quietly while you sifted my hair through your fingers.

I return to my post. The club is quieter now. The students in my program all come outside. They're discussing an assignment due Monday. They skirt around me.

"Hey," I call out after them. "You're welcome for letting you in." But they don't hear me. I exhale in frustration.

Jason sticks around, darting in and out of the club, updating me on what's happening inside. Two of the Navy guys leave with Kumiko's friends. Half an hour later, the third Navy kid leaves alone, looking dejected. The minor celebrity is carried out, her slack limbs hoisted by her struggling handlers. Puke dribbles from her mouth, and I grimace. Jason points at her and shrieks, and I elbow him when her handlers glower at us.

The two hours before the club closes are the hardest for me to stay awake. The sky casts these indecisive hues, as if the night can't decide whether to stay or go. And it's pretty much the same with the thinned-out crowd. Hooking up is still on some of their minds, but the bravado they had when they set out for the club is by now largely gone. Some of them linger so they can avoid the problems they left at home, but what do I know about that. When day finally breaks, when the last of the clubgoers stumble out and slide on their sunglasses, Jason comes bounding out and trots straight toward me. In the morning light, his shirt is even more turquoise.

"Let's get breakfast," he says.

Suddenly, I want him to be anywhere but here. I'm repulsed at the thought of spending any more time with him. He's my only friend in the program, but somehow this isn't enough to keep my vitriol at bay. He's firing away about whether he should have pancakes or a beef bowl when I blurt out, "Don't you have any other friends to bother?"

His eyes are wide and pure and filled with confusion.

"Huh?"

"I think you should try to make other friends besides me," I explain, though I already feel my face reddening with regret.

"Why would you say that?" he says.

My resentment has dissipated now, and I scramble. "I just need some time to myself."

"Then just say you'll pass on breakfast," he says incredulously. "You don't have to dump me as a friend."

He's right, but I've already dug myself into this hole, so I press forward.

"I just don't know why you want to be friends with me," I mumble.

"So what if I do?" he says. "What's wrong with that? And why do you keep pushing people away? Someday people will stop trying."

When I say nothing, he throws his arms up in disgust. "Fine. I'll leave."

He shakes his head and walks toward the train station. When he reaches the end of the street, he turns around.

"You're lucky you still get to be my roommate," he shouts, then disappears around the corner.

When I turn back toward the club, I see Kumiko standing there. She approaches me, and I wonder how much she just saw. She looks as if she's considering something. Then she speaks.

"Did you know, Andrew-kun, that needing help is not a sign of weakness?"

The pain of hurting Jason is starting to hit me.

"But what do I know about that," she adds. She wraps her arms around my neck and announces, "I'm not ready to face my husband. You are taking me out right now."

I'm not ready to face Jason or anybody else, either.

We walk to Azabudai Hills. Kumiko purchases tickets for teamLab, which has transformed the basement of a skyscraper into a vast labyrinth of technicolor madness. In one room, schools of iridescent fish, glowing yellow and silver, glide between us, beneath our feet, then leap into the ceiling, out of sight. In the next room, a kaleidoscope of shimmering butterflies, lime and gold and turquoise and coral, flit around us before dispersing into the dark. In another room—a massive lifelike aquarium—we're directed to draw cartoon sea creatures with colored pencils and crayons. We place the drawings under a scanner; moments later, holograms of the creatures we drew drop into the aquarium and interact with the hundreds of fish other visitors have drawn. I draw a sea turtle that wears Captain America's helmet and carries his shield. Kumiko draws a yellow Pikachu jellyfish with red, circular cheeks and the widest smile of any living being in the museum. We watch Captain America Turtle and Pikachu Jellyfish come to life, darting and bobbing and spinning in this teeming ocean.

I turn to Kumiko, whose face is awash in blue light. She is quiet, and her expression is inscrutable. We watch our turtle and jellyfish flicker in the water.

"Come on," I say quietly, extending my hand. She clasps it, and we make our way to the next room, and the next.

We exit and head toward Hamamatsucho, where we find a cluster of karaoke places. We reserve a small room and collapse onto the couch. The room is dark and reduces us to silhouettes. Song catalogs lay scattered on the table. The TV screen at the front hums in hibernation. There's a knock on the door, and a server enters; beer and cocktails are half-off until noon, he says. We order coffee, and he disappears. We lie down and fold into each other's arms. We're still alone, but for now, we're alone together.

When we wake up, two hours have passed. Our silhouettes are faint in the darkness of the room. Our two cups of coffee on the table are cold, and the TV hums and waits patiently for us to input the music. We stand groggily and stumble outside.

Rain is falling over Tokyo. I wrap myself around Kumiko, and she shivers when we step out from under the awning into the glistening street. We hunch forward and make our way to the train station. At the platform, we face each other. She wipes at the rain on her forehead.

"Why go back to him if he makes you feel this way?" I say.

"It's not that simple," she says.

"Can we see each other again?"

She smiles that tired smile. She's so tired, her eyes are practically shut. So are mine. She leans in closer and whispers, "I had a wonderful time, Andrew-kun."

And she is gone, lost in the sea of passengers rushing to catch the train.

An hour later, I'm back at Kamisoshigaya. It's noon, and when I enter the dorm, I'm greeted with the sound of raindrops plonking heavily on the metal roof. Everyone is asleep. They must be recovering. Sure enough, I open the door and see Jason on top of his covers, snoring lightly. He's still wearing his turquoise shirt. I stand over his bed. I tousle his hair, gently so he doesn't wake up, but he stirs, and his snoring intensifies, and I know I won't be getting any sleep after all.

I slide my hand into my pocket. I take out the origami crane, crushed and soggy and limp. I perch it on my desk, prop it upright. When I take my fingers away, it sags back into its formless shape.

I strip off my shirt and lie down. The rain outside is coming down even harder. Back home, when I was cocooned in a blanket in my van on nights like this, the sheets of rain would obscure everything beyond the windshield and pelt the roof so hard I felt I might drown. On those nights, to be honest, I would lie awake hoping my parents weren't doing well, either, wherever they were. And when I woke in the morning, exhausted, the realization would hit me that if I didn't manage to get out of there, I really would end up drowning, one way or another.

You got really sick. You took extended leave from teaching. Mrs. Jacobs would come to class disheveled and confused, and one day she stopped lecturing and asked if we might help her fold origami cranes. Of course, we said yes. Anything to get out of doing our assignments. She showed us the steps and the precise creases, and we spent the next four days folding cranes, and when we had a thousand, we strung them into leis, and she thanked us and said you certainly must get better now. Except you got worse. And toward the end, when it was clear you weren't going to make it, we asked Mrs. Jacobs what would happen with all the cranes. She looked at us kind of funny, and she smiled, something we hadn't seen in months, and she said, "Why, they'll help carry Mrs. Matsumoto into the constellations, of course."

* * *

I notice this tear that's made its way off my cheek and onto the pillow, where it disappears into the terry cloth.

She picks up just before it switches to voice mail.

"I told you not to call."

"Do you want to meet again? Tonight?"

There's a long pause.

"Tonight?" she says.

I'm not sure if she's still there, but then I hear her exhale.

"Andrew-kun. We need rest."

I look out the window. Rain crashes onto the windowsill. I hear Kumiko's breathing, slow and deliberate, its ebb and flow making me drift elsewhere.

"I miss you," I say, so quietly I'm not sure if I said it at all.

I delivered the paper cranes to you at the hospital. It was late morning, the Dayton skies were cloudless, and sunshine streamed into your room, revealing wrinkles on your face and neck and arms. You were connected to this machine by all these tubes. Mrs. Jacobs and I sat on the edge of your bed and strung the leis around your neck. You'd always wanted to visit Hawaii, you said, clutching the leis, your voice throaty and firm.

"My students worked hard to make these," Mrs. Jacobs declared.

"They just wanted to get out of learning." You laughed.

"And Mrs. Jacobs wanted to get out of teaching," I added.

"That's true," Mrs. Jacobs admitted.

Eventually you dozed off under the buoyant weight of a thousand paper cranes. Mrs. Jacobs and I watched your chest rise and fall underneath your hospital scrubs as the sun filled your room with light. And when you woke later, startled and alert, Mrs. Jacobs and I were there, beginning to doze off ourselves in the warmth and silence in that room.

GYM RUT

The fight at Infinity Gym starts over a machine Dirk thought was unoccupied. This powerlifter guy leaves it to go to the bathroom, and by the time he returns, Dirk has pushed the powerlifter's water bottle to the side and claimed the machine. Dirk says, "No problem, I didn't know you were still on it," but when Dirk overhears him mumble "Shouldn't it be fucking obvious," he flips right around and marches back to the powerlifter and says, "Is that right?" They grow belligerent, inching closer and closer, and by the time Jeff sprints across the gym floor from his manager office yelling, "Everybody, let's relax, let's all calm down," the two muscle-clowns have peeled off their tank-tops, their sweat and spittle spattering the other's forehead.

Dinesh, old and retired and pleased as punch, frowns as he snaps photos of the shirtless boys with his phone.

"Come on," I say to my client, Ann Jackson. "Let's finish up in the stretching room." We pretend to hulk out and we growl menacingly, and then we laugh as we make our way to the back.

I step into Jeff's office after I finish training Ann. He's slumped in his chair, hands clasped behind his head. The placard on his desk says *Hi! How may I help you?* When he sees me in the doorway staring at the sign, he flips it over.

"You OK?" I ask.

His suit hangs on a rack in the corner.

"Who's the interview with?" I ask.

"Some marketing company," he says. "But the longer you work at a gym, the less seriously people take you."

"Good luck anyway."

"How about you, Dominic? When are you getting a real job?"

I shrug. In the window behind Jeff's desk, I can see my reflection. It helps to have a nice body when you're trying to make a living as a personal trainer.

It also helps being twenty-six, and tonight's a packed house at Ménage, where, at the far end of the bar, I'm regaling a college girl with the play-by-play of how I subdued the two biggest guys at the gym.

"With pure logic," I say. "I reasoned them into submission." I pound my fist into my palm, as if to suggest that my method was in fact less diplomatic than that.

Her eyes widen.

"Which law firm do you work for again?" she asks.

I buy her another drink, even though I can't afford it.

"You look very tense, Dominic."

I'm waiting for my client at the front desk when Dinesh, the retiree, sidles up and strokes my arms. His palms are gnarled and warm, and flecks of his scaly skin sprinkle my arm like Parmesan. I jerk back.

"Very tense," he confirms.

"Just tired."

He looks at me, all businesslike. "I can arrange a massage," he says.

I smile politely. "I'll think about it," I say.

When he walks away, Dirk comes up and drapes his arm around my shoulder and whispers into my ear, "You look very tense, Dominic."

I shove his arm away and tell him to fuck off.

"So tense," he says. "You should get a massage."

"Chill. I work here," I say, but he does not hear me over his braying.

* * *

In the dumbbells section, the powerlifter guy approaches Dirk. The excitement level in the gym spikes to a thousand, and everybody pretends to focus on their own workouts when actually they're honed in like GPS systems to the two brutes. Jeff crouches forward in his office, hands gripping the edge of his desk, coiled as though ready to fire off from a starting block and sprint across the gym floor to the finish line. Dinesh raises his phone camera.

The powerlifter and Dirk exchange words, and Dirk follows him to the bench. Dirk helps him lift the dumbbells into position, and with that, everyone has lost interest. Jeff reluctantly sits down, disappointed, as though he's been robbed of something.

Ann bursts through the entrance, still in her work suit, towing her briefcase and gym bag.

"Sorry I'm late," she says. She quickly hugs me before rushing to the locker room, yelling that she'll be ready in three minutes.

Ann is several years older than me and one of my most dependable clients. She got her law degree from Northwestern, and she's since been blazing her way up as a public defender, but she's never made me feel subordinate. If anything, over the years that I've known her she's taken on the role of an older sister, celebrating with me when I got my first pay raise, scolding me when I handled a breakup heartlessly. People of her stature intimidate me, but I've known her from the start, so I yell back at her to hurry up.

For the next forty-five minutes, I make Ann work extra hard. By the end, her t-shirt is drenched, and after the final exercise—lunges around the perimeter of the gym—she drops and lies spread-eagle on the ground as she heaves and reminds me how much she hates me. I remind her that I'll see her on Friday, and tell her not to be late this time. I help her to her feet; her cool sweat makes me shiver when we hug. I tell her how proud I am of her for not quitting.

"Screw you," she says.

* * *

For the rest of my night, I train other clients. I try to sweet-talk Mrs. Rogerson, the seventy-two-year-old first-grade teacher, into actually doing her workout, but she insists on telling me everything there is to know about her cats and her arthritis and to ask about my romantic life. "That was wonderful. See you next week, Dominic," she says, and I wave her out the door. I have Dylan squat and deadlift while his mother waits at the juice bar. Dylan's trying to make his middle school football team. I tell him he's well on his way, and he puffs out his chest with excitement. Brittney, a student at the local university, slogs through her workout in frosty silence. She's twelve days away from her physique competition, and she hasn't eaten a carbohydrate in months. When we're done, I tell her she's going to do incredible. She finally cracks a smile, and she hoarsely confesses that she'd kill for spaghetti and a whole apple pie, and I say it's only twelve more days, Brittney, and then she covers her face and sobs.

I take my job seriously, but it wasn't always this way. College graduation snuck up on me, and I walked out the gates, diploma in hand, with no clue what to do next. Clouds rolled in heavy and deep that night, and it stormed through the next morning. I woke up the next day and decided to become a personal trainer. I gave myself six months to find a better job or get accepted to law school. That was five years ago. Somewhere along the way, I lost sight of the future, and I realized one day that I hadn't applied for a job in years and that I'd forgotten why I'd wanted to go to law school in the first place. Success was now measured by how many new clients I signed up. Unable to afford the lifestyle my college friends enjoyed, bankrolled by sparkly office jobs in the city, I saw them less and less, until they stopped texting me altogether. I was hurt, but I was also relieved. Now I didn't have to tell their corporate friends what I did for work.

Ménage is packed, and I'm waiting at the bar when I feel someone's hands on my shoulders.

"Ann?"

"Fancy seeing you here."

Before I can tell her that this is not a good time, the girl I'm with returns from the bathroom. She and Ann exchange a stare, and the girl asks Ann who she is.

"I'm Dominic's client," Ann says warmly. "I came by to say hello."

The girl smiles, relaxing.

"So, you're the one who keeps Dominic stuck in his cubicle all day," she says.

I sneak a look at Ann. Her face is unreadable.

"I wonder where he finds the time to get a body like that," the girl muses. "You'd think he spends all day at the gym, right?"

"It was nice meeting you," Ann says to the girl. "See you Monday, Dominic."

I don't reply.

"In your *office*," Ann says.

"Right."

"Are you embarrassed to be my trainer?" Ann asks the next day.

"Of course not."

"Serious question. I need to know."

Dirk butts his way into our discussion. "I work at Panda Express," he tells me. "No shame in what we do."

"Go away, Dirk," Ann says.

He grins and walks off.

"If you're embarrassed to be my trainer," she continues, "that makes me feel self-conscious, and I'd rather just work with someone else."

"I'm not embarrassed."

She stares at me with these narrow eyes before letting it drop. "If you ever think about changing your career, let me know, OK? I can help."

I imagine trying to come up with the money for this month's rent and car payment and student loans without Ann, then squash the thought.

"I swear I'm not embarrassed," I say. My hands are actually shaking.

* * *

When Jeff calls me into his office just before lunch, he has this tortured expression. His eyes are shut and his arms are folded over the desk, as though he's in the midst of a painful meditation.

"What's wrong?" I ask.

Now he looks constipated. When he opens his eyes, he doesn't look directly at me, just says, "I received a complaint about you."

"Me? From who?"

He shakes his head. "It's Dinesh."

"Dinesh? Why?"

"He alleges you displayed abusive behavior toward him, that you've created a toxic environ— . . . look, Dom. We both know this is bullshit. But I need to follow procedure."

"I didn't do anything wrong."

"I know that. Are you willing to have a talk with him? Smooth things over?"

"No way."

He sighs. "Just stay away from him for the time being, OK?" he says. "Whatever state of mind he's in, he'll eventually get over it."

"But I do stay away from him. He's always bothering me."

Jeff looks exhausted. "I'll speak with him. You just keep doing what you do, all right? I need you at your best. You bring in good business."

On my drive to Panda Express for lunch, I try to pinpoint whether my bitterness is directed at Dinesh, who I never wanted to know in the first place, or at Jeff, for treating the complaint seriously, or at myself, because I should have spoken up, and I've never once had the balls to. I grip the steering wheel so hard it loosens from the steering column, then I remind myself to go easy. The last thing I need is another bill.

I'm in line when I see Dirk working behind the counter. Our eyes lock before he turns away. He places the bowl of beef and broccoli on the counter and whispers into the ear of his manager, who looks at the clock. "See, you *are* embarrassed," I say as Dirk walks off and disappears into the back.

* * *

It's Jeff's birthday, and he's agreed to let me buy him a beer. I don't know how old he's turning. Maybe because he spends his days surrounded by younger people, he describes his age qualitatively, evasively, never providing an actual number. "I learned life gets better, not easier," he'll say. Or: "I'm just grateful to have the things I have."

I'm guessing he's thirty-nine. He looks fantastic, though. All that running around breaking up fights at the gym.

It's a slow night at Ménage. A group of women, all in pantsuits and blouses, have corralled the roped-off section in back. They occasionally erupt in laughter, but otherwise I can speak without raising my voice. We stand at the bar in the front and raise our frosted mugs.

"Happy birthday to my favorite manager," I say.

"I'm your only manager," Jeff says. "But thanks."

Our mugs clink, and I savor the cold bitterness and the distance from the gym and its head-splitting music and occasionally insufferable patrons. Jeff also seems to be enjoying the solitude. He stares serenely at the shiny bottles that line the wall behind the bar.

I'm about to order the next round when—

"Dominic? Jeff!"

Ann, in her navy pantsuit, makes her way toward us. She hugs us and says how happy she is to see us.

"It's Jeff's birthday," I say. "You're welcome to join us—in fact, we'd love for you to join—"

"It's my boss's birthday, too," she says. "You guys should join *us*." She points toward her coworkers in the roped-off section.

The reticence on Jeff's face mirrors my own desire for quiet, so I say, "Aren't you having a girls' night?"

"No. Well, yes. But join anyway?" Ann says.

Jeff shrugs.

Sensing victory, Ann grabs our hands and pulls us away from the bar.

"You'll love my coworkers," she says. "They're so much fun."

"Who do you work for again?" Jeff asks.

* * *

In the back, five women are sprawled out on a large sectional. Half-empty bottles and watery ice buckets and dozens of glasses litter the center table.

"Girls, this is Jeff and Dominic. It's Jeff's birthday."

They cheer.

"Happy birthday, guy. How old are you?"

Jeff's face reddens. "I'm just grateful to have the things—"

They boo, drowning him out. A woman thrusts glasses into our hands. Not just glasses, but flutes. Another woman approaches with an enormous champagne bottle, a brand I've never heard of. Bollinger. She pours some into Jeff's flute, letting it overflow and spill to the floor. When she pours mine, she does the same thing.

They fire off questions.

"What do you fellows do?"

"That sounds fun! What are tips for toning muscle and losing fat?"

"Never mind, that's too much work. Do you basically live in the gym?"

"Here, drink more."

Jeff peers longingly at the bar. For a second, guilt flashes across Ann's face, and then her coworker hands her a fresh flute of champagne.

"Hey. You."

The oldest and most senior-looking woman—the birthday woman, the one holding court—is motioning for me. The woman next to her makes room, and I take a seat. The birthday girl smiles. She has clearly been going hard all night.

"So, you're Ann's trainer?" she slurs. "Good lord, you're handsome. Can I feel your stomach muscles?"

Ann and her coworkers laugh uncomfortably. Several hoot tepidly before their voices trail off.

I don't want to embarrass Ann, so I lift my shirt. The birthday woman whistles and edges closer. I feel the moist heat of her breath on my neck. She slides her fingers over my abs. "Good lord," she marvels. The others have stopped talking, but she is oblivious. I don't know whether I feel like Michelangelo's David or a goat in a petting zoo, but when I see the look on Ann's face, I say, "Goat, definitely goat."

"Did you call me a goat?" the woman purrs, rubbing my chest.

"What?"

"Take off your shirt." Her eyes glint in the dark room.

Ann, looking tortured, stays silent.

"Relax," the woman says. "We're just having fun." Raising a nearly empty bottle, she says to Jeff, "Be a sweetheart and go find our server, will you?"

Jeff stiffens.

She looks at me again. "About that shirt."

Before I can decide what to do, Jeff stands and grabs me by the elbow and yanks me away.

"We're done," he says.

"We're just playing. Lighten up," the woman says, but Jeff tightens his grip and quickens our pace.

I wave back at them, and Jeff swears at me.

We exit Ménage. My face is burning, and the night wind whisks away the heat.

"You OK?" I ask.

"This is why I don't do birthdays," Jeff says. Then, "Fuck this."

"Dominic. Jeff."

We're almost to our cars when I turn and see Ann running after us, her heels clipping the pavement. Jeff doesn't stop, and I speed up alongside him.

"Wait," Ann calls out.

Jeff stops, and I crash into him. "Sorry," I say.

She catches her breath and crosses her arms.

"Jeff, I'm sorry, it was stupid of me, I should've let you enjoy your beer in peace, and Dominic, I have no idea where that came from, and if I knew she would act that way, I wouldn't have had you guys join. I am really, really sorry."

I'm about to say it's not a problem when Jeff presses his hand to my chest.

"Ann, here's the thing," he says. "Dominic and I work at a gym. We scrub toilets when the custodian calls in sick. What people in your profession bill clients in one hour is more than what they pay me for three *days* of work. What were you expecting? That your coworkers would ask to swap business cards?"

She considers this, opens her mouth, and then seems to change her mind.

"For what it's worth," she says, "I've never thought of you guys as anything less." She walks back toward Ménage. The click of her heels fades away.

Jeff watches Ann disappear inside before resuming his march. I jog to catch up.

"You OK?" I ask.

He slows down. "I shouldn't have blown up like that," he says.

"It's Ann. She understands."

When we reach our cars, he says, "Do you know what happened in there?"

"Sure. I got objectified."

"But do you know why?"

"She was drunk and she thought I was handsome."

He shakes his head. "What happened," he says, "was that lawyer wanted to demonstrate to everybody—you, me, her lackeys—that she was in total control. You and I, we're service workers, and so we were her perfect prop." Seeing me dissenting, he lifts his finger. "Do you think she would've done that to you if you worked at Google?" he asks.

"Yes."

"*No,* Dominic. No, she wouldn't have."

"She might've."

This makes him grimace. "Those turf fights at the gym over machines, you think they're really about the machines? Dinesh offering you massages when he knows you're not interested—do you think he actually believes you'll change your mind? Dirk making a joke of everything and everybody? Everyone's attempting to convince themselves that they alone are in control."

"I don't know."

"Yes, you do. Isn't this why you lie about being a lawyer when you try to pick up women at the bars?"

I don't reply.

"So just become one already, so you don't have to lie," he says.

"I'm happy where I am."

He chuckles. "When you're forty-seven like me and still eating ramen noodles, I promise you won't be."

"You're forty-seven?"

He ducks into his car. The ignition sputters before the engine starts. He looks at me through the open window.

"It's too late for me, but you still have time."

I don't reply.

"Thanks for the beer, bud," he says, and I watch him drive off.

"Dominic."

It's late afternoon and it's raining. I just completed my session with Ann.

"What's up?"

"There's an opening at my agency for a paralegal. I thought you'd be interested. It's a good start for people considering law school."

I don't say anything, and she continues.

"I went ahead and spoke with my boss, and she'd like for you to come in for an interview."

"Is she going to ask me to strip?"

Ann grimaces.

"She feels terrible about that. She doesn't know what got into her, and she wants to apologize to you in person."

"I don't care."

"I know you don't. But come in for that interview?"

"Let me think about it," I say.

"What's there to think about?"

"I'm comfortable with where I am."

She considers this. "Just don't get too comfortable," she says.

* * *

Dinesh stops me at the entrance. "I heard you're looking for work," he says. "I can pay well."

"For what?"

He doesn't answer, and I leave him standing there at the front desk.

That night, in bed, I flip through *Law School for Dummies*. Ann handed it to me on her way out. On the first page, it says *I know you're not a dummy, heck, you surely can't be,* and I slam the book shut and toss it into the corner.

I reach for my phone and reread Ann's last text:

Come on Dom. Take a chance. Have faith.

I think of Jeff's parting words today: *Go for it. Have faith in yourself. Nothing would make me prouder.*

I flick off the lights. In the dark, I remind myself I would not have met Ann and Jeff had I done life any differently.

I have faith.

The day of my college graduation was sunny and humid. The storm hadn't come yet, and the stadium was filled with excited parents in wraparound sunglasses and sundresses and short sleeves. I sat with my friends on foldout chairs in the middle of the field. I told a bad joke, and they laughed anyway. Our diplomas in hand, we vowed to remain close, though the promise felt dubious, even then.

That night we celebrated at Ménage. The storm rolled in while we were inside, and the streets became slick with rain. The wet sidewalks glistened orange in the streetlights. Inside Ménage, the bass thrashed, the strobe lights spun and cast a papery blue mist over our flushed faces, our sweat-darkened shirts. The beat dropped, our fists sliced the air, the possibilities were infinite. We drank our way to oblivion. One by one, we staggered out into the rain. Tomorrow, we'd wake up and face a new world. We'd be unstoppable.

III.

LOVE MAGNIFICENTLY

GOOD LUCK, CHAMP

I'm backed into the corner. Pain lances my knees. The featureless shadow approaches, backlit by halogen lights. He holds his chair high. I close my eyes, feel the heat of fatigue through my eyelids. What I wouldn't give for this to be the end.

But that's not in the script. In three, two, one—*now*—I vault to the side, sending Kolache Kaden's chair clanging into the ring post. He howls, his voice high and tremulous, so it comes out more like an indignant squeal.

"You suck, Kolache!" someone shouts from the crowd, prompting a chorus of lusty jeers.

Beneath his scowl, Kolache's eyes crinkle with embarrassment, but I have no time for sympathy. I scamper behind him and snatch the chair from his hand. He whips around, confused and distraught. He rests a fist on his hip and scratches his head. This stirs the audience into a frenzy. Kolache Kaden can't be faulted for lack of showmanship.

"Mister steal yo chair, steal yo chair," they chant, filling the Dayton High School gymnasium with bloodlust.

For a moment I allow myself to bask in the adulation. As I raise the chair, Kolache falls to his knees and clasps his hands together.

"Noooo, Raging Rick," he wails.

"Yes, Kolache Kaden," I growl. I circle the chair high in the air, count backward, then carefully slam it down, ostensibly aiming for his face.

I freeze for a moment when the chair makes contact and flattens Kolache. I toss the chair, put him in a gentle headlock, and bend forward, concealing our huddled conference.

"What the hell, Kaden, you were supposed to roll away."

He is hysterical. "I know I'm sorry I forgot what do we do now oh god that really hurt."

"Skip to the end," I whisper. I lift him to his feet and send him stumbling. He smashes into the post, then covers his face, as though this day couldn't get any worse.

The crowd goes wild. "Finish him!" they scream.

I launch Kolache into the rope. He rebounds and rushes toward me, concentrating so hard that I can't help but be impressed, before he dives and lands safely on the floor of the ring. He springs up when I turn, tackles me, then twists my legs and drives his weight into my shoulders. The referee slaps the canvas three times, and it's over. Kolache Kaden, against all odds—odds made much worse by his own ineptitude—has defeated Raging Rick.

"Did I do good, Rick?" he whispers excitedly, his weight still bearing down on me.

"Get off me. Go to the ref. Just go."

The audience is stunned, their applause scattered and tepid. Based on Kolache's loopy grin, one would think he'd won the world championship belt. I lower my head onto the canvas and shut my eyes. Who is he kidding. This is the Dayton Wrestling Circuit. This is high school gymnasiums at thirty-eight years old. This is sixty-five dollars a match and no one ever wins.

Noah's awake when I get home. He sits before the television, swaddled in blankets and gripping the PlayStation controller. At his side,

Helen frowns at the screen, then curses and tosses her controller. Buying him the console for his seventh birthday last year was my idea.

"Who exactly are we getting this for?" Helen had asked, and I shrugged and grinned.

"Dad!" Noah cries now, looking up from the screen. "I stayed up for you."

"You should be in bed, champ."

When they're finished pulverizing zombies, I hoist him off the couch and embrace him. Wisps of what hair remains shimmer under the pale living-room light. Compared to Kolache, he is as weightless and limp as a teddy bear scooped of its cotton innards.

"Did you win?" Noah asks.

I swing him over my shoulder, thinking carefully. "Well, champ. There's a couple of ways to look at this. When you consider the long-term implications, it becomes apparent—"

"You lost?"

"It was practically on a technicality."

"That's OK, Dad. You'll win next time."

At the kitchen table, Noah blathers while I shovel down tangles of spaghetti. Helen smiles at him and swishes a tea sachet in circles.

"So can I come to your next match?" he asks.

My fork hovers midair. Helen catches my eye and shakes her head.

"Sorry, bud," I say. "We need you to get stronger first."

The chemo has nearly wiped out his white blood cells.

Noah pouts for only a moment. Then he's chattering again.

"I'm going to be a wrestler when I grow up," he informs me when I tuck him into bed.

"Is that right?"

"Or a zombie hunter."

"Let's stick with wrestling." I bend down and kiss his forehead. "Go to sleep, champ."

I kill the light. Through the darkness, I see the outline of his tiny brave form burrowed underneath the blanket. Then I shut the door.

"We need to talk," Helen says in the living room.

It confounds me that four syllables can induce so much stomach acid.

"I've run the numbers. I need to take on more shifts."

Helen is a nurse, and she reduced her hours to care for Noah, though these days that mostly means keeping him company indoors. Before he got sick, he was a whirl of dashes and somersaults and treasure excavations with his plastic shovel in the backyard, and he'd only reenter the house on Helen's third and final warning.

"Even if I get picked up by the national circuit?"

"How soon can we expect that?" she asks, gently.

Alvaro, the circuit commissioner, has promised me a title shot in seven months, which will surely get me noticed by the national players. He has every match planned out until then, including tonight's loss to Kolache and a forthcoming string of losses, before I surge into a winning streak. I imagine Noah's excitement when he sees me hoist the title belt.

"Not soon enough," I admit.

"Noah will be happy to have a better zombie-shooting partner."

I wonder if Helen's patience has a cap, if she'll one day realize she can do so much better. I grit my teeth, as though I could chew the thought away.

Her mouth curls into a smile. "Eh, I like you enough," she says, reading my mind. "On most days."

"Careful. You're talking to the future Intercontinental Champion."

She laughs, then apologetically covers her mouth, but it's too late. I lift her off the ground and powerslam her into the couch. She shrieks with laughter, then glances toward Noah's bedroom door and presses a finger to her lips.

"Don't make me pile drive your ass," she whispers, which is Noah's favorite move, and I imagine a day I cannot pull that finisher for him, and now Helen is clutching my shirt and shushing me.

"Steady, Rick," she is saying. "It'll be OK. We'll get through this," and I'm not sure that we will, but she holds me anyway, to keep me from drifting to a place from which there is no return.

In the morning, I back the ice cream truck carefully out of the driveway. The job has its perks. I get to sit all day, which helps me withstand the abuse in the ring, and it provides an endless supply of Choco Tacos to get me through the nights after scheduled losses, or through the weeks following Noah's chemo treatments, when he remains in bed for days, only getting up to vomit. In the fall, I sell Dippin' Dots from a kiosk by JCPenney at the Fairfield Commons mall. In the winter, it's hot cocoa and roasted peanuts.

Seventy-seven-year-old Mabel Rogerson, my first-grade teacher at Southeast Dayton Phase Two Elementary School, waits for me at the first stop. She waves frantically when I turn the corner.

"Stop," she cries. "Stop right here."

I lean out the window. "Good morning, Mrs. Rogerson," I yell. "I see you."

"Stop at once!" she commands.

I slow to a stop and jump out of the truck and hug a beaming Mrs. Rogerson. "How is my favorite Daytonite doing today?" I say.

We stand on the sidewalk as she peels the plastic off a fruit bar.

"How is Noah?" she asks.

He looked so peaceful this morning. He didn't see Helen and me standing over his bed, his silent protectors unable to protect him. We watched his chest rise and fall with every breath.

"He's hanging in there."

"How about you, Rick?"

"I'm great. I have no idea what I'm doing with my life."

"You definitely don't."

A couple in their twenties, faces hidden behind oversize sunglasses, push a stroller past us on the sidewalk. I step into the road to make way.

"Good morning, Mrs. Rogerson," they say.

"You both look fabulous today," she says, and then jams the fruit bar into her mouth.

They disappear around the corner.

"Mrs. Rogerson, do you ever imagine how your students might end up as adults?"

"All the time. Helen turned out well."

"What did you imagine for me?"

"Feeling needy today, are we?"

"Very."

She considers this. "Rick, you turned out exactly how I thought you would."

"Well, damn."

"You were destined to be the best father Noah could hope for."

"Did you actually pay me a compliment, Mrs. Rogerson?"

She smiles. "I feel a big number two coming. At my age you treasure these moments." She hands me her barely eaten fruit bar. "Be kinder to yourself, Rick," she says, before slowly making her way back inside.

Two months ago, after three years of traditional surgeries failed and the doctors laid out what few options remained—options they themselves were skeptical of—Helen and I sat at the kitchen table and faced off.

"There's no evidence this will work," she said. "And it might make things worse."

"What choice do we have?"

She said nothing.

"You're saying we should give up?"

"It's the worst form of leukemia, Rick. He's sleeping for most of the day. If there were any chance, you could count me in. But this is a fool's game. Please."

She reached out her arms, but by then I was on my way out the door.

I stayed in my truck that night, furious at Helen's pessimism. The next morning when I came back in, she was still at the table, and I wondered if she'd been there all night. I approached cautiously, but before I could apologize, she wrapped her arms around me.

"I don't know what to do," she said.

Sunlight sifted in through the blinds.

Holding each other, we stumbled into the bedroom and collapsed on the bed, our eyes following the whirl of the ceiling fan. Eventually we drifted into a restless slumber to the sound of Noah obliterating zombies in the living room, saving our world from certain doom.

After work, we convene for practice in Alvaro's basement. We take turns in the ring he's set up while the rest of us run through our routines on mats lined up along the cinder block walls. On Friday, I'm scheduled to lose to the Grim Preacher, who in real life is Father Toby Bekkum, my childhood friend and assistant pastor at Saint John's Episcopal. In the ring, he wears a faux clergy robe. When he wins, he raises his arms and then huddles over the loser, praying for forgiveness. When he loses, he does the same, but sprawled on the floor and clutching his cross. We can never figure out whose forgiveness he's praying for. The audience adores him, as do the other wrestlers and his congregation.

Toby and I sit cross-legged in the corner, haggling over the components of our routine. "You can dropkick me here, but I'm going to suplex you there," I say.

"No backbreakers," Toby says. "I have a wedding that day. Also, I need to mow the church lawn."

He's wearing sweat pants and a t-shirt, and his hair is pulled back with a headband. I'm relieved he's not in his wrestling clergy robe, which he hasn't washed in weeks. We run through transitions, but we've been doing this for years, so there's not much to practice. We soon plop down on the mats and watch others bungle their routines.

"How's Noah?" he asks.

"He's hanging in there."

In the practice ring, Sergeant Swagger powerslams Kolache Kaden. Toby and I wince when Kolache lands completely wrong.

"Why would you ever land like that?" Sergeant Swagger asks, mystified.

"Obviously I didn't mean to," Kolache retorts, rubbing his hip.

"I do Wednesday services," Toby says to me. "Come. I'll run a collection for Noah." He notices my hesitation. "Come for the collection."

Swagger and Kolache are arguing now. The other wrestlers stand by, grinning, ready to pull them apart.

My gratitude outweighs my shame, but not by much. "You should really be praying for Kolache Kaden," I say.

"Even the church has its limits," he admits.

On Wednesday, Father Toby Bekkum waves to us from the pulpit as Helen and I slide into a pew at the back. I sit stiffly in a collared shirt and slacks I haven't worn in years. My neck and waist stretch the seams, my feet ache in oxfords that haven't left my closet in a decade.

"Folks," Toby says. "You all know Rick Delaney. Come out this Friday and watch us wrestle with honor."

"Raging Rick!" someone shouts from a pew in the front.

"Tonight's collection is for Rick's family. We know they can use our support, so let's show them that Saint John's love."

Collection plates are passed around, and the congregation cheers when the worship band strikes up my entrance theme song: Faith No More's "Epic," a nineties alt-metal hit. Father Bekkum winks at me. *For Noah,* he mouths, and I begin to crumble, but Helen slips me her hand, and I straighten up and square my shoulders. I have my menacing stage reputation to protect.

"Tonight," Toby says after the collection, "I want to talk about our decisions, decisions that make or break us. I want to talk about when our own understanding isn't enough."

Helen leans forward. She's been a keen listener for as long as I've known her. A former high school wrestler herself, she was dubious at first when I told her my dream of becoming a professional wrestler. I'd come home one night with a swollen ankle from a bad fall, and when she questioned whether it was worth the risk of getting injured just to participate in a scripted act, I rushed to the sport's defense.

"It feels unscripted when you're actually in the ring," I insisted.

She taped my ankle. "How does that feel?" she asked.

It felt better already.

"How does that feel?" she asked a feverish Noah, years later, as she placed a cold towel on his forehead.

"Can I sleep with you and Dad tonight?" he asked.

Helen and I exchanged looks, neither of us excited about a fever ball kicking us all night.

"Of course," Helen said.

I stifled a sigh. Sure enough, he kept us awake, though now I wish I'd been a better sport.

As Father Bekkum speaks, he waves his arms animatedly, then widens them, as if to embrace the congregation.

"We should come more often," Helen whispers. "Toby is so good."

"So good," I say, resting my eyes, wishing I were home with Noah, who by now has probably cajoled his babysitter into shooting zombies with him. I try to push away the thought that we wouldn't be here if I had a better paying job in the first place.

For the first time that I can recall, Mrs. Rogerson isn't waiting for me when I turn the corner. I idle at the curb, then honk. I shut off the ignition and walk up to her door. Her next-door neighbor is standing in the yard, watering potted flowers. She approaches when she sees me knock.

"Mabel suffered a stroke last night. She's in the hospital," she tells me, clutching her bucket.

"Is she all right?"

"I don't know."

I dash to the truck and scoop up every fruit bar from the back.

"Can you keep these for her?" I ask. "Tell her it's from the ice cream truck guy?"

She hesitates. "You do know Mabel doesn't like ice pops?"

The bars are softening in my hands. "I did not."

She smiles sadly. "Give your son a great big hug tonight, OK?"

"Why can't I come?" Noah asks. He slumps at the kitchen table, arms crossed, head dug into his chest.

"I'm sorry," I say. "Your health comes first." I tilt his head up. "You're my good luck, champ. No matter what."

Noah seeks a second opinion. "Mommmm."

Helen lowers her fork and rubs her temples. "You know what? We should go."

Noah's arms shoot up.

"Helen," I say quietly.

She nods tiredly, seeming reluctant. "It's the right thing," she says. "You guys are partners in crime, after all."

Noah slices his fists through the air, clearly not listening to Helen's admonishment that he'll have to keep his mask on at all times. Amid the excitement, I nearly forget that I'm slated to lose to the Grim Preacher.

A swath of Father Toby Bekkum's congregation waves placards for him from a far section of the gymnasium. PREACH, GRIM PREACHER, one reads. FATHER BEKKUM! CAST ALL YOUR ANXIETY ON HIM BECAUSE HE CARES FOR YOU. I wonder who the placard is referencing. Not to be outdone, a cadre of my former schoolteachers has commandeered a front section and wave handmade signs. RAGE, RAGING RICK! RAGE AGAINST THE DYING OF THE LIGHT. Another reads: RICK! I AM YOUR FATHER. From the locker room entrance, I scan the gymnasium for Mrs. Rogerson. Of course, she's not here.

I frown when I spot Noah with Mr. Mossinger, his second-grade teacher, who's sitting in Helen's seat. I jog up to them.

"Noah, where's your mom? Hello, Mr. Mossinger."

"Hello, Rick. Helen asked Noah to keep an eye on me for a bit. Isn't that right, Noah?"

Noah is playing a shooting game on Helen's phone. He looks up and points toward the side door. "She went that way, Dad," he says before returning to the game.

I make my way toward the door, stopping for photos and handshakes along the way. A gust of night wind sweeps past when I open the door. "Close the door, Rick," someone calls out from the crowd. I step outside and wait for my eyes to adjust to the dark.

In the distance, beneath the soft glow of the streetlamp, two figures sit on the curb. I recognize Helen's outline and begin to approach, but halt and take refuge behind a tree when I hear her words.

"I still don't understand," she is saying.

I hear Toby's voice, but I can't make out his words.

"Noah doesn't have time, Toby. This would mean everything to him."

I slide farther behind the tree. Toby murmurs.

Helen retorts, "You two can wing it and it'll look more real than any match with Kaden."

Toby's voice rises. "This would destroy not just my wrestling career but Rick's as well," I hear him say. "We can't change things that have already been decided." His voice softens, and his words vanish.

"I don't know." Her voice hardens. "I don't know. I don't. I'm tired."

They are quiet, motionless. Mist rises under the light of the streetlamp.

Toby stands, and she takes his proffered hand. I hunch in the tree's shadow and hold my breath as they pass by and disappear into the gym. I wait for a minute, then follow them inside.

A year after we married, Helen and I celebrated our anniversary at Applebee's. We told the hostess why we'd dressed up, and she congratulated us and told us to save room for dessert and then winked. I informed her that Helen's favorite was the Triple Chocolate Meltdown.

Toward the end of dinner, two young boys approached our booth, their father trailing behind.

"Raging Rick, can we take a picture with you?" the taller one asked.

I assumed my stage persona, clenching my jaw and squinting.

"Here, I'll take it," Helen said brightly, reaching for their father's phone. "Smile, boys."

I scowled into the camera.

I told them to study hard and listen to their parents, and sent them on their way, then apologized to Helen for the interruption.

"You're not sorry," she replied. "You love it."

I grinned. This was shaping up to be a fantastic anniversary.

"It might take time for me to get noticed nationally," I said, more to myself. "But I'll get there."

The breadsticks and Alfredo had settled nicely in my stomach, and I felt the first coils of drowsiness. The chatter from the surrounding booths blended into a pleasant din, and across from me sat a creation far too divine for a plain denizen of Dayton like me.

Helen grabbed my hands and squeezed them. "Time," she said, "is something we have."

Through the locker room doors, I hear the crowd's muffled boos for Kolache Kaden and cheers for Sergeant Swagger. Toby and I sit and wait on opposite benches. His head is bowed, his eyes closed, and his lips quiver as he clutches the cross that hangs from his neck.

He lifts his head and looks at me. "Rick," he says, lowering his cross. "I was just praying for your family."

"We'll be fine."

"God is on your side, my friend."

"Sometimes you're really annoying, Toby."

"What?"

"I meant, it's really annoying that one of us has to lose."

"I pray we can all be winners. But in some ways, I suppose we are."

"What have I won?"

He smiles sanguinely. I'm imagining ripping off his chain and shoving the cross up his ass when the doors swing open and Kolache charges through, with Sergeant Swagger behind him.

"I *told* you the DDT was a bad idea," Swagger says. "You don't have the flexibility."

Toby stands. "Everything OK, gentlemen?" he asks.

"Oh piss off, Toby," Kolache says, storming past us.

Toby raises his arms. Kolache and Swagger disappear around the corner. A moment later, we hear Kolache sobbing.

Toby grins and extends his fist. "We're up. Let's give them a helluva show, Raging Rick."

Hot static prickles my skin the moment I swing open the doors and sprint toward the ring. The Grim Preacher, foreboding in his robe, paces in the ring.

"Raging Rick! Raging Rick!" the crowd cheers.

I slow to a stop when I reach Noah and Helen, both of whom wear somber expressions.

"You *have* to win, Dad," Noah pleads.

I clasp his shoulders. I can almost feel his bones give way. "You'll be my good luck, champ?"

He squares his chest. "I'll do my best."

"I know you will," I say, my voice cracking, and I wink and give him a thumbs-up.

I walk to the ring and flip over the rope. The crowd roars. I squint at the Grim Preacher. Any trace of his warmth in the locker room is now gone.

The bell sounds. We circle the ring, our hands suspended in the air like praying mantises. The Grim Preacher makes the first move and dives for my knees. I sidestep him, wrap my arms around his robe, and slam him into the ground. He snatches me by my trunks and flips me onto my back, grunting as he presses painfully into my shoulders. He rams my head into the soiled canvas, saturated with sweat. Noah's screams pierce through the crowd's rumble. I peer out into the stands and lock eyes with him. *I'm fine,* I mouth, just before the Grim Preacher's boot crashes onto my head. For a moment, I'm blinded by an explosion of stars.

Noah had been complaining of dizziness for a week when one night after dinner, he stood from the table and swayed like a car dealership Gumby on a windy day, before he collapsed. We rushed him to the hospital, where they ran a series of tests that lasted until the next month.

The night before the diagnosis, Noah tossed in the hospital bed in a pool of sweat. Helen and I sat by his side all night long. He woke in the morning after having finally fallen asleep a few hours earlier, his eyes tired and wide.

"Am I in the hospital?" he said, his voice breaking.

"We're all here together," Helen said, stroking his hair.

"Can I have Cheetos?"

I sprinted to the cafeteria and emptied the vending machine.

"I wanted *one bag*, Dad," he said on my return, and we laughed, and for a moment, I allowed myself to hope.

I wriggle free from the Grim Preacher's choke hold, then knock him down onto the canvas. I regain my breath as he writhes and clutches his stomach. I stride toward him, then haul him over my shoulders. He squirms and scissor kicks as I rush to the ropes and fling him out of the ring and onto the gym floor. I dust off my hands and walk away, smiling as he roars with displeasure.

On the other end of the ring, I flip over the ropes and make my way to the sportscasters' table, where they've left a folding chair. The crowd's cheers intensify when I grab it and reenter the ring. The Grim Preacher struggles to climb after me. I conceal the chair behind my back and calmly wait for him to squeeze through the ropes.

He stands and meets my gaze, and we begin the countdown. Four. He steps toward me, ignoring the chair behind my back. Three. He quickens his pace as I step back, bracing myself. Two. He dashes forward as I raise the chair high over my head.

One.

The Grim Preacher tumbles to the right. By then, I've turned in the same direction. His eyes widen, and I slam the chair onto his head with all my might. The crowd gasps as the chair crashes with a splintering crunch. He falls back onto the canvas, the blood sluicing from his forehead and darkening the ring in an expanding pool.

Toby stares up at the rafters, stunned. His eyes swivel toward me. "What are you doing?" he says, dazed.

And then it is silent. The world hovers, suspended.

"Where are you, Dad?"

I had cornered myself in an alleyway with no escape. Noah and I had gotten separated outside the town library. Before me, a swarm of zombies advanced, their arms suspended in the air. I cocked my assault rifle.

"I'm a block east, Noah. There's ammo in the gas station. Don't worry about me."

I aimed and fired and took down the first row of zombies, who fell to the pavement, their spindly arms raised toward the orange sky. The row behind took their place and marched forward.

"I'm coming, Dad. Stay alive."

"Save yourself, Son. The gas station."

I aimed and fired, but I had run out of bullets. I lowered my rifle. I was doomed.

"I'll save you, Dad. I will. I will."

Behind the swarm of zombies, Noah leaped from around the corner, his body sheathed in impenetrable armor. He raised his machine gun to his eyes, which had narrowed into slits, barely visible under the shadow of his helmet. "Back. Off. From. My. Dad."

I dropped the controller onto the couch and reached over to Noah sitting beside me, his gaze trained on the screen. I adjusted his chemo cap.

He swatted my hand away. "Dad, I'm *saving* you."

I pulled my hand back. "Indeed, you are," I whispered.

For a moment, the living room was silent, and then the plates on the table clattered with the thunderous rapid fire of his M2.

The chair dangles in my grip. I face the crowd. Helen covers her face, leaving slits for her eyes. Noah punches the air. *Let's gooo, Dad,* I see him yell, though I cannot hear him over the roar in my ears.

Toby is silent. His gaze follows the ascent of the chair. His hands are clasped. He clutches his cross, as though praying for forgiveness. As though praying for deliverance.

DO NOT RESUSCITATE

The first thing Ann Jackson notices when seventy-seven-year-old Mabel Rogerson—Ann's first-grade teacher at Southeast Dayton Phase Two Elementary School—calls this early Sunday morning is how weak her voice sounds.

"Is everything OK?" Ann asks, her voice fraught with concern.

"I'd like you to come by." Mabel's words are barely audible. "Please."

"Oh my god." Ann panics. "Say no more."

During the nine-minute drive to Mabel's home, Ann replays in her mind how, just three days earlier, she had notarized Mabel's advance directive—a document Ann wrote herself—a seemingly innocuous favor for her favorite teacher. Mabel had recently returned from the hospital after having suffered a stroke, and she stated, in no uncertain terms, that if something dire were to happen again, the doctors were not to administer any life-sustaining treatment. Ann is not an estate lawyer—she is a public defender of the state—and drafting this directive, she felt guilty and uncomfortable.

When Ann's knocks go unanswered, she cautiously twists the doorknob and finds it unlocked.

"Mrs. Rogerson?"

Ann pokes her head inside. The living room is dark and musty and smells faintly of antiseptic. Two cats perch on the embroidered sofa, staring at Ann with narrow eyes. The oak dining table is set for one, plates and utensils neatly laid at the head. The heavy curtains are drawn, letting in just slivers of silver sunlight. Silence blankets the room.

"Hello?" she calls out again, then makes her way down the hallway.

The cats swivel their necks, following her with their eyes. She peeks into the room to the left and sees Mabel on her bed, slumped under a mess of blankets.

"Mrs. Rogerson!" Ann rushes into the room.

"Oh, Ann," Mabel whispers hoarsely, her eyes shut. In her green floofy pajamas, she looks both ancient and childlike.

"I'm here!" Ann kneels by Mabel's bedside and places a hand on her shoulder. "What is it? What can I do?"

Mabel remains silent for nearly a minute. When she finally speaks, she does so haltingly. "My dear Ann," she says. "Will you look after my cats when I'm gone?"

Ann cries out. "Oh no, Mrs. Rogerson, oh no no no. Oh god how long do you have until you are. . . . gone? This is awful."

The words *do not resuscitate* flash in her mind like night district neon lights. Her eyes well up. She should never ever have notarized Mabel's advance directive. What was she thinking?

"Four days," Mabel murmurs.

"No!" Ann screams.

Mabel sighs deeply. "The calico is Killer and the tabby is Hoedaddy."

Ann wipes her eyes. Memories from first grade with Mrs. Rogerson flood her mind: story time with deeply satisfying, deeply happy endings, treasure hunts leading to full-size chocolate bars for the entire class, rainy afternoons spent creating ladybugs and jellyfish with the brightest, thickest construction paper.

Ann pauses. "Why on earth would you name your cat Hoedaddy?" she asks.

"Because he's a ho," Mabel whispers.

"Oh." Ann's unsure how to respond. "I see. Well, I will make sure Killer and . . . Hoedaddy are loved and cared for." Ann sobs. "I love you so much, Mrs. Rogerson."

Mabel's trembling lips curve into a thin smile. "I love you, too, sweetheart. Now I'd like to get some rest."

Ann smooths out the blanket over Mabel's tiny body, then quietly shuts the bedroom door. On her way out, Ann passes by the cats; their eyes shine like steel flints in the darkened room. Of all the lessons Mabel has taught her, in this moment, Ann thinks of the time she and her first-grade classmates pestered Mabel for nearly an hour, asking every question they could come up with, and how Mabel patiently answered everything, forgoing whatever lesson she'd planned, and how, afterward, when they finally ran out of questions, Mabel surveyed her class, brimming with pride, and told them to always, always stay curious.

Later that morning, unable to focus on anything else, Ann peers at her vibrating phone and gasps at Mabel's name on the screen. Ann leaps out of her chair.

"Do you need me to come over?" Ann asks breathlessly.

"Come over?" Mabel's voice is bright and chirpy. "No, I'll swing by tonight and drop off the keys for when you feed the cats."

"Feed the cats?" Ann says. "Aren't you dying?"

"Who's dying?" Mabel asks, startled.

"You are."

"I'm going to die?"

"Yes. You told me. You'll be gone in four days." Ann's voice cracks. She collapses into her chair. Her eyes brim with tears once more. She vows to never sign an advance directive again. Oh, Mrs. Rogerson!

In the silence, Ann hears her own labored breathing.

When Mabel speaks, she does so carefully. "I'm leaving for Honolulu on Thursday for five days of sun and mai tais and shirtless hula boys. Is that what you're referring to?"

"What—"

"Oh my."

"—the hell, Mabel. You looked like death this morning."

"Oh, that!" Mabel says brightly. "I was up all night watching Maury Povich reruns."

Ann doesn't say anything.

"And I might have had a tiny bit too much to drink," Mabel adds.

Ann remains silent.

"It was actually a lot," Mabel admits. "I had some bourbon left in my flask, and I also found this lovely cabernet in my pantry, and also—"

"OK, OK. Oh god, I was so worried."

"I suppose I could have recovered from my hangover before summoning you," Mabel concedes. "I'm sorry. I just wanted Killer and Hoedaddy to meet you before I set them loose on you. You know how cats can be."

"Mrs. Rogerson?"

"Yes, sweetie."

"Just don't leave us for good anytime soon, OK?"

"Ann, dear."

"Yes?"

"This town will have to burn me at the stake to get rid of me."

For as long as Ann can remember, she's possessed a hyperactive imagination that, while helping to keep her preoccupied during her childhood years of ostracization from her classmates, also frequently brought with it immeasurable anxiety from the preposterous scenarios she concocted. In the third grade, her teacher showed the class a documentary about the Bermuda Triangle and the countless lives that had supposedly been lost in it. Ann could not sleep for weeks. She was convinced that the Bermuda Triangle would find its way to Dayton and swallow her whole. She feigned sickness for days, terrified it would find her on her walk to school, until Ann's mother, her patience long gone, shoved Ann out the door and ordered her to school, then chain-locked the door. Ann sprinted to school, convinced that as long as she made it into the school building, she'd live another day. She vowed to outrun the Bermuda Triangle for as long as she needed to, which lasted for three weeks, when her teacher showed the class a horror movie about a Babysitter and the Man Upstairs, at which point she had far more dire things to worry about. It was only decades later that the thought crossed her mind that maybe this teacher was a terrible person. Why had she shown this movie to Ann and her classmates in the first place?

Years later, law school at Northwestern followed by four years of working in Big Law in Chicago had instilled in her a healthy sense of cynicism, but still, Ann never lost her propensity to take something innocuous and blow it up to magnificent proportions. Just last month, when her younger sister, Hailey, announced she was unexpectedly returning to Dayton, Ann, though relieved to hear this, worried why Hailey was coming back suddenly, why now? Had Hailey discovered she was terminally ill? Was she escaping a deranged ex-lover?

Later that week, at her mother's home, Ann tells Hailey about Mrs. Rogerson. She starts from the beginning, telling Hailey and their mom, Patricia, that Mrs. Rogerson had asked her to write up an advance directive, and how that eventually cascaded to Ann receiving the scare of her life. Hailey's eyes light up when Ann describes the advance directive, but she remains silent and attentive.

"What was I even thinking?" Ann laughs. "I can be *sooo* dense," she says in closing.

"Advance directive?" Hailey says. "You can write one for me, too?"

Her eyes are bright, but her skin is sallow, her hair stringy, and her weight far too low. She's looked like this since the day she returned home last month, her military kit bag nearly the same size as her, or so it seemed to Ann when she saw her baby sister for the first time in years as Hailey emerged from the security checkpoint at O'Hare.

Today, at the dining table, Ann grimaces. Patricia stiffens. They are sitting, the three Jacksons, over coffee and a platter of chicken nuggets Patricia has microwaved to a nuclear crisp: just the way her girls used to like them. An unopened carton of cookies-and-cream ice cream waits in the freezer.

"I would like an advance directive, too," Hailey says. "Just in case."

"Just in case what, honey?" Patricia says flatly. She bites into a nugget, nearly cracking her dentures.

Hailey shrugs. "You never know. One moment you're here, the next moment a sad drunk driver can mow you down on the streets, you know?"

"Sweetie," Patricia says, turning to Hailey. "You need one of those as much as I need new teeth." She rises from the table, and her dentures take this opportunity to fall out of her mouth. She curses, but the words come out more like a painful gargle. She fits the dentures back into her mouth.

"I thought so," Hailey says. "Ann, will you please—"

"Who wants ice cream?" Patricia interrupts. "We all need ice cream. You girls stop talking. I'll be right back." She disappears into the kitchen.

"How's work?" Ann asks, eager to shift the conversation.

Hailey shrugs. "Same old. How's it with you?"

"Same. Can I come visit you sometime at your store?"

"I'm not sure my boss would like that," Hailey says. Then, "Sure, why not."

Patricia returns with spoons and bowls filled with cookies-and-cream. "Well," she says. "Here's one thing I can eat safely. Ha!"

"I'll swing by one day," Ann promises Hailey, and then the three of them focus intently on their ice cream, as shame engulfs Ann.

And Ann is thirteen, in the thick of seventh grade. Her routine is to do her homework at the public library, a twenty-minute walk from home. She doesn't have any friends, but ballet classes and schoolwork keep her busy.

On Saturday mornings, after ballet, Ann stuffs her backpack with textbooks and trudges to the library, where she stays long after she's completed her homework; surrounded by so many wonderful books, she has no desire to go home.

One Saturday morning, Hailey follows Ann out the door. Hailey is seven and has yet to display interest in reading, but she is loyal to Ann.

"Go back home," Ann tells her without slowing down. "You won't like it there."

"I want to be with you," Hailey says, trotting to keep up. "Slow down," she pants.

Ann does not slow down. In fact, she picks up her pace. By the time they reach the library, Hailey is gasping for breath.

"I have to use the bathroom," Hailey wheezes.

Ann sighs and leads her to the library bathroom, then picks a seat at an unoccupied table and spreads out her books. Minutes later, Hailey joins her, jumping in her seat and tapping the table.

"You need to be quiet," Ann whispers.

Hailey quiets down for a moment before resuming her jumping and tapping. "I'm bored," she whispers.

Ann puts down her pencil. "Hailey," she whispers. "If you go home right now, I promise I'll play with you for the rest of the night once I'm back."

Hailey's face brightens. "Really?"

"Shhh. Yes. But you have to go now."

Hailey hops out of her seat. "OK! See you soon!" She waves excitedly at Ann, then dashes out of the library.

Ann sighs with relief and returns to her homework. She completes it in less than an hour. She puts her things away and walks to the Young Adult section and peruses the books. She picks out the conclusion to a trilogy she is excited about. Within minutes, she's lost in postapocalyptic Chicago, only looking up hours later and realizing she should go home.

When Ann returns, Patricia looks up from the sofa. "Where's your sister?"

"I sent her home hours ago," Ann says.

"From where?"

"The library," Ann says.

Patricia leaps up, her face filled with panic. "The library? That's a mile and a half away. And it's been hours."

"She's not a baby," Ann says.

"She's *seven*."

Patricia dials the local police, and now she's reporting Hailey as missing, and honestly, Ann doesn't think it's that big of a deal, but she knows better than to say anything at this point. Patricia's hysterical now; at one point, she drops to the floor, her sobs guttural and feral and filling Ann with shame.

That night, the police return a tear-stricken Hailey into Patricia's arms. Hailey got lost and wandered off to a playground, where she hid, terrified, in a plastic slide tunnel for hours until a young family discovered her and brought her to the police.

Patricia grounds Ann for six months; during that time, Ann is barred from the library.

"It's OK," Hailey says brightly when Ann apologizes. "Now we can play together more," she says, and this breaks Ann's heart.

And Ann is sixteen, Hailey ten. It is four months before they'll cease ballet lessons for good. They are at the Dayton Community Center, dancing in what will be their final performance, though neither of them knows it then. Ann, along with the girls and boys her age, is on the stage. Patricia sits in the audience. Hailey is in the back room with her age group, practicing their routine one last time.

Mr. Monetti, their instructor, has chosen a Bolshevik number for Ann's group and choreographed a routine that's too difficult for them. They've rehearsed for months, but on stage their performance crumbles, and they look like the disheveled, surly teens that they are. When they finish, the applause is muted. Mr. Monetti stands stiffly, stone-faced, on one end of the stage. But Ann has more important things on her mind. Her high school guidance counselor recently identified her as a high-performing student and will do what she can to help Ann get accepted to the best schools. Ann is ecstatic. Ballet, already a middling priority, is pushed to the back of her mind.

Ann changes out of her costume with relief, then joins Patricia, who pats her daughter's knee consolingly, as if Ann actually cared.

For Hailey's age group, Mr. Monetti has chosen a more appropriate number: the theme song from the *Harry Potter* movies. The audience sits higher in their seats the moment the music begins. These kids are talented, unlike Ann and her angsty dance mates, and even among this group, Hailey stands out. Her movements are precise, confident, her demeanor poised. The performance ends to rapturous applause. The kids smile and wave, blow kisses to their families.

On the drive home, Hailey says she can't wait to move up to the next age group, that she's looking forward to dancing with Ann. Patricia reminds Hailey of how proud and excited she is for her. She's excited for Ann, too, she adds, a definite afterthought. Then they are quiet, and Ann thinks about how her life will truly begin once she starts college.

Four months later, Ann is seventeen and done with ballet. The truth is, she doesn't know why she stuck it out for this long. Patricia resists, at first, but relents when Ann reminds her what an acceptance at the University of Chicago would mean. The university would cover all the expenses that Patricia and Ann can't, which is nearly the whole cost.

Hailey, ten years old and still fervently loyal to Ann, promptly quits ballet, too, much to Patricia's disappointment. Ann feels guilty, knowing how much Hailey will miss it. But her college applications come first, so she stays quiet.

Even though Hailey is only ten, it's clear to everybody that she doesn't have an aptitude for school. She's struggling in the fifth grade. She's embarrassed, but she digs deep and doubles her efforts.

"I wish I was smart like you," Hailey confesses wistfully to Ann one night, unable to finish her homework.

"Just keep studying," Ann tells her. Her mind is elsewhere. She is taking the SAT in two months. She is nervous and excited. Years of being willfully ignored by her classmates, of walking unnoticed through the school hallways—none of that will matter the moment she starts her new life in Evanston, or Ithaca, or Hanover. In the back of her mind, she's aware that she could be helping Hailey. But she has so much on her plate, and there is so much at stake.

And Ann is twenty-four, in her final year at Northwestern Law School, returning home for Hailey's high school commencement. Ann has recently accepted an offer from one of Chicago's most prestigious law firms, and she is excited and distracted. Still, she stands and cheers wildly when Hailey's name is called.

Afterward, the three of them celebrate at Applebee's. They do not talk about the fact that Hailey isn't going to college. For now, they are all quietly relieved that she has made it through high school.

Three months later, Hailey starts working at Fairfield Commons in a store that sells teen apparel. Her supervisor is seven months younger than she is. Hailey keeps her head down and does a decent job most days. She lives at home with Patricia, who loves Hailey dearly but fears that she is going nowhere in life, much like how Patricia's own life has turned out.

And Ann is twenty-eight, living in Dayton once more, now working for the state as a public defender, having gotten fed up with the grind and politics of corporate law. Her first assignment is to defend Bert Reyes. On a horrific night that rocked the city for months, Bert's father, Angelo, known to everybody in his neighborhood as a gambling addict, returned home frenzied after a night of excessive drinking and staggering losses. Though Bert and his mother were intimately familiar with his violent behavior, on this night, Angelo came home particularly unhinged and at one point pulled out his firearm and threatened to kill Bert's mother. Bert, convinced that his father would actually shoot, jumped into the fray. After a struggle, he wrested control of Angelo's firearm and shot him in the abdomen. Angelo died two days later.

Brand new to public defense, Ann finds the case daunting and overwhelming, but she does her best. So much is at stake.

Hailey, now twenty-one, still works at the mall. One day during her lunch break, after getting reprimanded yet again by her supervisor, Hailey wanders into the Armed Forces Hub on the lower level. The recruiters convince her that she'll have no future if she stays here in Dayton. Her only shot to make something of herself is with them, they say. They tell Hailey things that she has always felt to be true, but this is the first time she is hearing them out loud. The words should feel like a slap in the face, but they instead feel cathartic, confirming that her place in life is exactly where she has suspected all along.

Half an hour later, she enlists with the Army, then goes upstairs and promptly quits her job. Six weeks later, Hailey is shipped off to basic training at Fort Benning. Patricia cries every day for weeks.

Five months later, Hailey and her brigade are deployed to Kabul. When Hailey schedules video calls with Patricia, Ann drives to her mother's home, even if the call is during work hours, and even if she is in the middle of something important for Bert's case. During one call, Ann and Patricia scream when they hear gunfire erupt. The video feed ends abruptly. Ann and Patricia do not sleep until Hailey emails the next day and tells them she's fine.

A month later, Bert is found guilty of second-degree manslaughter and sentenced to five years in prison. Bert receives the verdict coldly, then turns and stares at Ann.

"I did my best," Ann whispers.

"But did you?" Bert whispers back, sending chills through Ann, because she isn't entirely sure.

She promises Bert she'll work to secure him early parole. On the day he begins serving his sentence, his face is filled with so much despair that Ann can't sleep for a week.

Nine months later, Hailey returns to Dayton for good, medically discharged from the Army and unwilling to speak about her time overseas. Though Patricia and Ann are relieved to discover she's physically unhurt, they soon understand that her medical discharge is no fluke; Hailey has come back with crippling depression and anxiety, which make Ann and Patricia scrutinize Hailey's every move, ready to spring into action at the first indication that she might harm herself.

Hailey gets her old job back, and her life in some ways returns to how it was before she enlisted: she lives at home in her childhood bedroom, she puts in four shifts at the store every week, and Ann, who lives twenty minutes away, visits them when she can.

And though Ann isn't living the life she expected, she vows to carry on anyway, driven by her ambition, or what remains of it, and a growing sense that she somehow continues to fail those who need her the most.

Ann can't bear to remain in the office any longer. Bert will be released on parole in four days, and if she's being honest with herself, she doesn't know what to make of this. Ann should be ecstatic—she worked for two years to make this happen—but something about his early release doesn't sit right with her.

She knows that prison has inflicted psychological damage. When Ann finds the time, she visits Bert and keeps him abreast of her latest efforts on his behalf. She still feels the weight of guilt; Ann is confident her present-day self could have gotten Bert a sentence of less than a year, if not an outright acquittal. And over the course of these visits, she has witnessed Bert's alarming decline. She sees in his eyes a wild, shifty, discombobulated nervousness along with flickers of rage. Ann is very concerned. She recognizes that Bert needs to leave prison; at the same time, she isn't sure he's prepared for the outside world.

But what haunts Ann the most is her nagging suspicion that there might have been something sinister on Bert's mind, years ago, in the moments he shot his father. Most signs suggested Bert acted in self-defense, but the better Ann got to know him, through numerous conversations and then reflecting on these conversations while lying awake in bed late at night, she began to wonder if Bert wasn't so different his violent, abusive father. Ann left several of their meetings feeling disturbed and shaken and, frankly, afraid for her own safety.

In any case, Ann will pay him a final visit in two days to discuss the release proceedings, and she is dreading having to face him. She doesn't want to think about any of this right now. She shuts off the office lights and exits and drives to Mabel Rogerson's house, where the cats are waiting to be fed.

She finds Killer and Hoedaddy grooming each other in the dark. They freeze when the lights come on—Killer's tongue suspended on Hoedaddy's ear—and stare at Ann accusingly. Killer's ears flatten.

"Oh my god, *what*?" Ann says, throwing her arms up. "I just came to feed you. Do you want dinner or not?"

Killer slowly resumes his licking of Hoedaddy's ear. Hoedaddy's eyes have narrowed into slits.

"You know, I'm a very busy person," Ann reminds them. In the kitchen, she snaps the lid off a tin of beef liver. Moments later, they are by her side, purring and rubbing themselves on her ankles.

"Oh *now* you like me," Ann says, but she smiles as she dumps the contents into their bowls. It's quiet now except for the smacking of their mouths.

After they lick their bowls clean, Killer and Hoedaddy return to the couch, where they snuggle into each other. Minutes later they are asleep. Ann observes them, envious that they fall asleep so easily. It must be easy when you can sleep by someone you trust, she muses.

"Can I sit by you guys?" she asks the cats. She takes a seat on the couch. She grabs the remote and switches on the television. A historical war movie is playing, and the room fills with the rat-a-tat of a Gatling gun and the screams and groans of men collapsing onto the battlefield. She quickly changes the channel.

"How do you do it?" Ann once asked Hailey during a video call.

It was a week after the unexpected gunfire that had left Ann and Patricia petrified for three days.

"Do what?" Hailey said.

"Deal with what you have to deal with every day. Sleep at night after hearing all those terrifying sounds."

Hailey paused. For a moment, on Ann's screen, she looked just like the seven-year-old girl who'd followed Ann to the library. Ann could hardly breathe.

"I just pretend I'm someone else," Hailey finally said.

"You mean you pretend you're *somewhere* else?" Ann asked.

Hailey shook her head. "No. Someone else."

"Like who?" Ann asked.

"Sometimes I pretend I'm you," Hailey confessed. "Sometimes I pretend I'm a smarter, better version of myself. Sometimes I pretend that I stuck with ballet. I still miss it, you know." She paused. "And yes, sometimes I pretend I'm somewhere else, too," she conceded. "Like back home. With you and Mom."

Ann choked up. Her stress from her clients was nothing compared to the horrors her baby sister endured every day.

Ann jerks as soft fur shimmies on her leg. Hoedaddy has crawled into her lap.

"What the hell," she says softly, then strokes his back.

Hoedaddy curls into a ball and purrs.

"You are the cutest," she whispers.

A moment later, Killer crawls onto her lap and joins Hoedaddy. They jockey for position, then, finding positions satisfying to both, settle in for a nap. She alternates petting each cat.

"Can I ask you guys something?"

They ignore her, but she asks anyway.

"Do you think I'm as awful of a sister as I think I am?" She shifts her leg a little, causing Hoedaddy to open his eyes and glare at her.

"I'm so sorry," she says.

Killer lifts his head and licks her palm, the rough papillae scratching her skin.

Tonight they're celebrating Patricia's fifty-seventh birthday at Golden Peach, a tradition that began when going out for cheap Chinese was a luxury for the Jacksons. Dimly lit and with green laminate booths that haven't been reupholstered since the 1980s, Golden Peach is a place they always find comforting. Throughout college, Ann would return to Dayton to join her mother in the celebration. Their server, a glum middle-aged woman, takes their orders of sweet-and-sour chicken, orange chicken, and sesame chicken, selections that have remained constant for the past decade; they feel their server judging them, but the food is consistently delicious, and they are used to the less-than-stellar service. Here, they never feel out of place, surly waitstaff notwithstanding.

"Can I interest you in some chicken?" the server asks archly after taking their orders.

"Yumi!" her manager snaps from three booths away, but Ann smiles determinedly; she refuses to be upset for the rest of the night. She has had a rough day.

On the muted television screen in the corner, Bert's mug shot floats above two solemn newscasters; Ann's smile falters. The newscasters' mouths move grimly, talking, in all likelihood, about Bert's parole earlier today. Bert's face stares at Ann menacingly. Memories from this morning rush back. The sinking feeling returns.

Bert's mother informed Ann late last night that she was busy; could Ann pick Bert up from prison in her stead? Ann reluctantly agreed.

The release process was orderly and uneventful, much to Ann's relief. She led Bert to her car, where he silently slid into the passenger seat.

"Would you like to get an early lunch?" Ann asked.

"Sure, if you're that hungry," Bert answered.

Ann bristled. They drove the rest of the way in silence. When he turned to look out the window, she appraised him; she saw sallow skin, mottled hair, a deadness in his gaze. A wave of guilt and shame rose within her.

At Applebee's, they ate in silence; Ann regretted bringing him here. She should have taken him straight home so she could be done with this.

"Is it too early to ask what your plans are?" she asked toward the end of the meal. "For what comes next. After you rest, of course," she added.

Bert grinned. "I don't know. Maybe shoot up a school."

Ann gasped. "You shouldn't joke about that, Bert."

Bert's grin widened. "But am I joking? You should know. You're the lawyer, right?"

Ann froze.

His smile faded. "They told me I shouldn't have gotten any jail time."

"Who is they?" Ann whispered.

"Everybody." He picked at his pasta. "I don't know. I'm still disappointed, you know."

She rose. "Excuse me for a minute. I'll be right back."

In the bathroom stall, she worked hard not to hyperventilate. She covered her mouth and stifled a cry. She steadied her breathing and waited for her trembling to subside. She stepped out of the stall and studied her reflection in the mirror. She marveled at how much she had aged. She reminded herself that others have endured far more stressful situations than she has. Her thoughts shifted to Hailey.

When she returned to the booth, Bert was gone.

"Ann?"

Patricia and Hailey are staring at her with concern.

"Are you OK?" Hailey asks.

From a distance, the manager aims the remote at the television and switches it off, then nods sympathetically at Ann.

"I'm here," Ann says, quietly. Her heart pounds. She forces a smile. "I'm here," she says. "Let's eat."

It's a late Saturday morning at the office, and Ann puts away the documents and switches off the lights and locks up. She needs to stop coming in on the weekend. Always the overachiever, Ann has never learned to truly relax.

As she's leaving the office parking lot, she decides to visit Hailey at the mall. In the last couple weeks, Hailey has been awfully quiet, and Ann is concerned. She checks her watch. Hailey's store shouldn't be busy yet; it's before the afternoon rush. Ann hums in the car. They'll grab lunch at the mall, most likely somewhere in the food court, but maybe one of the full-service places. She'll ask Hailey if there's anything she can do for her.

She parks close to the Macy's and walks through the department store and takes the escalator to the second level. Swaths of shoppers bustle past.

As she approaches Hailey's store, she hears yelling. She peeks inside and sees two male customers berating Hailey at the checkout. Nightclub trance music blares from the ceiling speakers.

"I'm very sorry," Ann hears Hailey say, but the two customers continue chewing her out.

Ann stiffens. They have no idea what trauma Hailey has suffered, these two privileged men, and Hailey's coworkers don't seem interested in helping her out.

"I want to speak with your manager," one customer demands.

"I'm so sorry," Hailey says again. "The manager is on break. He'll be back in ten minutes."

The customer slams the counter. Hailey and Ann both jump.

"Hey," Ann calls out, marching toward the store, but as she's choosing her next words, she hears the unmistakable pops of gunshots fired in succession. She freezes. Hailey and the two customers freeze as well. In fact, no one in the store moves.

The stillness lasts for a couple of seconds. Then screams fill the mall atrium, followed by a stampede of people rushing toward the first floor and the exits.

"Oh my god," Ann whispers. She is standing just inside the entrance, behind a column, still invisible to Hailey.

"Oh my god!" one of the male customers yells.

"Run!" yells the other.

Everyone in the store rushes toward the entrance.

In the distance, the gunshots continue, along with screams and shouts, now joined by a wailing alarm.

"Hailey!" Ann yells, but a fleeing customer knocks her to the ground. She rolls to the wall and curls into a ball. She hears more gunshots and sirens in the distance.

"Hailey!"

When the stampede has passed, Ann struggles to her feet.

"Hailey!" she yells, rushing deeper into the store. The ceiling speakers continue to blare trance music. The store is abandoned.

"Oh my god," she whispers, turning and rushing out of the store.

In the atrium, customers sprint in every direction, and the alarm is still wailing. There's one more gunshot, and then only screaming and thunderous footsteps and the wailing alarm and a chorus of sirens approaching.

"Hailey!" She doesn't know in which direction Hailey went, so she sprints toward the center of the mall, away from the exits. She scans every panicked face that rushes by.

"Hailey!" She runs past store after store, all abandoned, except for the store selling sports jerseys and caps, where she sees a figure huddled behind a clothes rack, their hands covering their ears. She rushes in. It's a middle-aged man, who's whimpering quietly. She dashes back out.

"Hailey!" She is now in the center of the second floor of the mall. In the west wing, next to the store selling pretzels, she sees two bodies motionless on the ground.

Then she sees Hailey. Her baby sister is standing on the railing overlooking the first floor.

"Hailey! Get down!" Ann screams.

Hailey walks on the railing, arms extended, as though balancing on a tightrope. Her eyes are nearly closed.

"Hailey, please!"

Hailey raises her arms, points them toward the ceiling. She raises one leg, forming an arabesque.

"Hailey, what are you doing?"

Hailey lowers her leg, then buckles her knees, then jumps slightly, an assemblé.

Ann screams.

Hailey lands nimbly, her eyes still nearly closed, then swivels into a pirouette.

Ann steps toward Hailey, extending her arm. "Hailey, please," she whispers. "Let's go home."

Then the gunman appears from around the corner. Beneath his trench coat, he wears camouflage; the mask that conceals his face is camouflage, his boots are camouflage. His trench coat is darkened in spots.

"Hailey," Ann whispers. "Please."

He spots them. Changing course, he walks toward them.

Hailey spins, then hops, landing lightly on the railing.

And Ann is eleven, Hailey five. They are at Graeter's, the three of them, Ann, Hailey, Patricia, tackling an impossibly large banana sundae, a luxury. Patricia is the first to give up, though it crosses Ann's mind that maybe Patricia wants to make sure the girls get their fill. Ann and Hailey dig in with determination. The rush of sugar courses through their bloodstreams, making life feel impossibly hopeful.

"I love ice cream," Hailey declares, her flushed cheeks covered in whipped cream and cherry juice.

Ann could not agree more. Today, Ann understands, is the perfect day.

Ann gives Hailey one final smile, mustering decades of love for her baby sister. "I'm here," she says. She moves slowly, then picks up speed, until she is sprinting straight for the gunman.

In the foyer of the mall, the sound of a single shot fired.

MANUAL FOR HOW TO LIVE MAGNIFICENTLY

There's this little park nestled behind a row of quiet homes in southeast Dayton that Mark Dekker likes to come to. It has a swing set and a curving slide, and the lawn is blanketed with mowed grass that feels, under his bare feet, like cold velvet. If he comes at the right time, before the final bell for the day rings at Southeast Dayton Phase Two Elementary School and after the parents have taken their kids home, he gets the park all to himself. He comes here when he can't bear to stay inside his efficiency apartment but still wants to be alone and hidden from the world. Here, he sits on the swing until he gets bored, and then he walks back to his empty apartment.

It's a Wednesday, probably, maybe—he's lost track, but he'll figure it out before he gets ready for work. He's a server at Applebee's, a job he actually enjoys quite a bit, though it's not where he imagined he'd end up.

He's about to stand from the swing when someone behind him calls out, "Oh my! Is that Mark, the fortune teller? I would never forget a seer like you."

He sees a face he knows from Applebee's.

"Mabel Rogerson?" He's surprised he remembers her name after all these years.

"Oh my! You remembered me! What a hunk. Can I sit next to you?" Mabel climbs onto the swing and pumps her legs. "Yippee!" She swings vigorously. At the top of the arc, she releases her hands from the chains.

"I'm not a fortune teller anymore," Mark says, omitting that he got fired after less than six months. He begins to swing. "Actually, I'm not much of anything these days."

Mabel slows to a stop. "That's good. Fortune telling is the business of charlatans. You're better off doing anything else."

"Even serving margaritas at Applebee's?"

Mabel smacks her lips. "You're doing God's work." She studies Mark. "Is everything OK?"

It has been a month since the shooting, and a prevailing sadness lingers over the quiet town of Dayton. Plus, Mark is grieving in other ways.

"I wish I could be happier," he tells her. "I recently lost the most important person in my life."

"I'm so sorry," Mabel says. She lowers her head. "These are terrible times."

Mark halts his swinging. "I don't think I can go on without her." He feels numb. He stares past the edge of the playground. When he faces Mabel again, she is crying.

Mark stands, alarmed. "Are you OK?"

"Absolutely, sweetie," Mabel says. She inhales sharply. "I'm fine." She collapses onto the ground, and she covers her face with her hands.

Mark rushes to help her up, then changes his mind. He sits beside her on the ground. Gradually, Mabel's cries subside. They're alone in the park, Mark and Mabel.

"Sometimes I wonder if it's even worth it to keep going to work," Mark finally says.

"Some customers really need their Blue Hawaiian Long Island Iced Teas," Mabel counters tearfully. Then she adds, "And that person would be me." After another pause: "In fact, I could use one right now."

"Yeah, me too," Mark admits. He checks his watch. "I guess I should be getting ready for work." He stands to leave. "Will we be seeing each other again, Mabel Rogerson?"

Mabel shakes her head. "I don't think we will, young Mark," she says. She looks so tired. Then her face brightens. "Unless we run into each other at Applebee's, in which case you know what to do."

Mark raises a finger. "One Blue Hawaiian Long Is—"

Mabel raises two fingers. "*Two,* Mark. Two Blue Hawaiian Long Island Iced Teas. If we had three hands, we'd make it three Blue Hawaiians."

This is one of Mark's final memories with his mother. He has made them breakfast: bacon, scrambled eggs, and coffee. He is no cook. They're sitting on the porch. It's dark, and it's raining lightly. She thanks him for breakfast but leaves it untouched. She no longer eats much, but her spirit remains intact, at least when she's lucid.

"Promise me you'll find somebody, OK?" she says, meaning a girlfriend.

"What is my name?" Mark asks.

"It's Mark, you silly. Now promise me."

"It's not like I haven't been trying."

"You've wasted enough time caring for me. Soon you'll have the time."

"Stop."

His mother smiles at him so tenderly that he turns away.

"Eat," he says, so she nibbles at the tip of the bacon, and his despair is so overwhelming that he covers his face.

She wraps him in her arms.

"Oh, my Mark," she says. "You don't know how lucky I am to have been your mother. Don't feel bad for me, OK?"

This makes Mark feel even worse.

She whispers, "Someday, when you're a parent, you'll understand."

Months later, on her deathbed, she calls for Chester repeatedly. And Mark says what he knows he has to. But that morning, as Mark and his mother have breakfast on the porch in the rain—in one of her final lucid moments—she doesn't hesitate to remind Mark that he is her son, and she is his mother. He will never, ever let go of this memory.

In the days after the shooting, the funerals for the seven victims were held in quick succession. Mark followed the news online, reading about the life of one victim after another, before his grief compelled him to turn off his laptop. The final funeral was for Ann Jackson, the thirty-one-year-old public defender who attempted to stop the shooter, and who, by all accounts, was the primary reason the carnage ended that day.

Mark attended the funeral. The church overflowed with mourners, and her casket disappeared under the mountain of flowers the community placed by her resting body. It was in stark contrast to his mother's funeral five months earlier, which had been simple and sparsely attended. At Ann's funeral, Mark sat in a pew in the back; from there, he now recalls, he saw Mabel hold Ann's mother up as she screamed relentlessly. At the mother's side stood a woman who could have been Ann's younger sister, shellshocked and mute.

Business at Applebee's was quiet for the first couple of weeks, and Mark and the other servers mostly stood around and scrolled on their phones. Luna, the bartender, mixed them colorful cocktails with a splash of alcohol, which the manager didn't object to. In fact, Mark once saw the manager whisper to Luna, and Luna poured more vodka into his drink, and the manager gratefully patted her shoulder. Mark was grateful to while away the time with his colleagues. He wondered if they, too, looked forward to seeing each other in times like these.

The media caravan eventually left, and then the customers began to return. Mark busied himself once again in the drudgery of taking orders for Bourbon Street Chicken & Shrimp and Triple Chocolate Meltdowns. Slowly, the crowds grew, returning almost to normal.

Tonight, the father and son in Booth Three are so festive and cheerful that Mark has asked them twice if they're sure they aren't celebrating a birthday. He's prepared to comp them desserts. They are Mark's first customers since the shooting to demonstrate such unbridled joy, and he wants them to savor the delights of the Sizzlin' Butter Pecan Blondie.

"We're sure," the father grins. "I'm just happy my son's home."

The son is tall and thin and serious and looks to be a couple years younger than Mark. He sports a crew cut and sits up perfectly straight. Mark is certain he is in the military.

"Are you happy to be back in Dayton?" Mark asks the son. He is genuinely curious.

"Like you couldn't imagine," the son says.

Mark tries to picture the exotic, wondrous places the son has been. Okinawa, perhaps? Italy or Germany? Mark asks him where he was stationed.

The son hesitates. "Creech, actually, forty-five minutes outside of Las Vegas," he says, and Mark's excitement deflates a little.

Mark takes their orders for a second round to the bar, where Luna deftly maneuvers about the rows of bottles and glasses and spritzers. Her hair is pulled back with a hair band. Faint creases of concentration form on her forehead as she fills both highball glasses at once. Mark can barely focus on one thing at a time, and sometimes even that is a struggle. She is three years older than him. If they were in high school, he thinks, he'd be a freshman, and she'd be a senior, a gap that would have seemed enormous back then.

"It's nice to be busy again," Luna remarks, catching Mark studying her. Luna is always businesslike. In fact, he can't recall if he's ever seen her smile. Not that she has a dour demeanor. But she always seems to be completely focused on her work, which also might explain why Mark has never seen her make a mistake, not even on the busiest nights.

He brings the Dark & Stormy and a gin and tonic to the father and son, who are engaged in a spirited conversation. Actually, it's the son doing all the talking. The father just sits there. He looks blissful. Mark sets the drinks down and leaves. His own father was absent even when his mother passed away. He doesn't feel sorry for himself, of course. You don't miss somebody you never knew. His thoughts turn to his mother, and he's pummeled with waves of grief. He sets his serving tray on the bar and stoops down and steadies his breathing.

Somebody squeezes his shoulder. He looks up and sees Luna extending a glass of Coke. Her gaze is impenetrable.

"You gonna be OK?" she asks.

He gratefully takes the glass.

"Holler if you need anything," she says, then steps back behind the bar. Within seconds, she's mixing more cocktails.

He vows to display a similar kind of resolve for the rest of the night and busies himself with his customers as professionally as he can. The woman in Booth Two orders a Blue Hawaiian Long Island Iced Tea, and he thinks of Mabel Rogerson. He grins.

"Excellent choice," he tells the woman as he slides the cold glass on the table.

He thinks of Mabel swinging in the park, her legs pointed toward the sky. He thinks of everything she's seen in her lifetime. Wherever she is, he hopes she's having a wonderful night with a nice drink by her side. In the kitchen, the cooks briskly prepare one platter after another of the popular entrees.

There's a commotion in the main dining room. Mark rushes out to see a man has joined the father and son. He's the same age as the son, and they're locked in a tearful embrace.

Mark slowly walks past their booth, careful to give them space but also a little curious. He's hoping to catch a tidbit or two, and he's rewarded when he hears the new guy say, "I never thought you'd want to see me again." The son says, "I'm sorry, Hannon," over and over again.

Hannon is a nice name, Mark thinks. If he ever has children, he'll name them Hannon if it's a boy, Helvetica if it's a girl. The father in the booth is beaming, his hands clasped smugly behind his head, as if he might be guilty of having planned for all of this to happen.

Mark whispers to the father, "So, let me offer that celebration dessert again."

The father chuckles. "You know what? We'll take it." He clasps Mark's hands. "I'm a really happy dad right now. I'm not sure if you can tell."

"I would've never guessed," Mark says.

The father closes his eyes. "Yep. I'm a happy dad."

Mark feels a mixture of loneliness and joy. "Let me go grab you guys that pecan blondie."

He makes his way to the kitchen. As he passes the bar, Luna looks up at him before focusing again on her work.

Back in his apartment, Mark sits on his couch in the dark. The glow from a streetlight outside the window dimly illuminates his silhouette. Three of the victims were kids between the ages of six and fourteen. Seven lives cut senselessly short.

During his short-lived career as a fortune teller, he discovered early that his audience loved it when he spewed clichés. All that glitters isn't gold. Forgiveness is a process. The whole reason clichés existed, he learned, is to make grieving people feel a little less bad; once he realized this, it was difficult to deliver these lines without feeling self-conscious and ashamed. And yet he finds himself sitting on this couch frequently telling himself it is better to have loved and lost than never to have loved at all. On some nights, he thinks this cliché is about his love for his mother, and that in spite of the pain, he is nonetheless grateful for the time that they shared. On other nights, he reminds himself it actually refers to romantic love, something he has little experience with, and something he needs to get working on, if only because he promised his mother he'd try.

He hears the soft patter of rain falling outside. He glances out the window. He already knows he'll be falling asleep on the couch. The first coils of drowsiness overtake him. Then darkness.

The two women have been sitting alone for an hour, in silence, at the long table in the middle of Applebee's dining room. Past the swinging doors that lead to the kitchen, deep inside a dark metallic fridge, is a cake that could feed twenty with Happy 50th Birthday, Yumi! piped in pink frosting, cold and untouched. Bright plastic sparkles and party favors and empty water glasses line the table. The younger woman looks humiliated, and the older woman looks glum.

As Mark approaches to refill their water glasses, the younger woman starts to apologize to the older woman again.

The older woman holds up her hand. "Harmony. Just *stop*," she says. "It's not your fault nobody likes me."

"I don't know what I was thinking, organizing this . . ."

"You were thinking of cheering me up, because I'm depressed. And I'm touched. But how about we just order and eat and call it a night. The food here is garbage, by the way." She glowers at Mark. He shrugs and fills their glasses.

"I'm so sorry, Yumi," the younger woman says.

"I said *stop*." She squints and traces her finger down the menu. "What's this nonsense about oriental chicken salad wraps?"

"Oh!" The younger woman's face brightens. "That one's not bad, actually."

"OK, Harmony, maybe you should add it to the Golden Peach menu, then."

At the bar, Luna is wiping the work counter with a washcloth.

"This is awkward," Mark says as he joins her.

"You mean them?" Luna asks, nudging her head toward the two women at the empty table.

"Yeah. I feel bad. Especially for the birthday woman. Imagine literally nobody showing up."

Luna shrugs. "That's how it's been for me my whole life," she says.

"You?" Mark says, doubtfully.

"You know," Luna says, pointing at her face. "My resting . . . blank face. It scares people away. I've always had it. Nobody ever wanted me at their parties. They said I could suck the fun out of any room."

Mark doesn't know how to respond.

Luna leans forward, across the bar. "Hey," she whispers. "Go tell them drinks are on me tonight."

"Really?"

"Our city needs to heal," she says, "one drink at a time." She winks at Mark and waves him off.

At the table, the two women are finally talking, to Mark's relief. It sounds like a very serious discussion.

"Actually, I just got promoted to Gold," the older woman is saying in a low voice.

"That's *wonderful,* Yumi," the younger woman says. "How exciting! One day you'll have to teach me how to play."

"I can teach you tonight," the older woman responds, her voice perking up. "I need a duo for ranked."

"Oh. Um." The younger woman's face reddens. "Uh, sure. Actually, I just remembered, I have to get back to my kid after this. Rain check?"

"I thought so," the older woman says, her voice flat once again. She looks up at Mark, irritated. "Yes?"

"Sorry," Mark says. He points at Luna. "The bartender would like to offer you drinks, on her."

"Why?" the older woman asks.

"To celebrate your birthday, of course," Mark says. He raises his order taker. "What can I interest you ladies in?"

"Oh." The older woman puckers her lips. "Well," she says. "In that case, I'd love a whiskey sour. Thank you for this."

"I'll have a Blue Aloha Mana Margarita," the younger woman says excitedly.

"Excellent choices," Mark says, as the older woman shakes her head disapprovingly at the younger woman.

Back at the bar, Luna says, "The whiskey's for the older woman, yes?"

"They asked me to convey their gratitude," Mark says. "They really did need some cheering up."

Luna twists the cap off a shaker. "I think we all do," she says. She fixes her blank gaze on him. "You holding up?"

"I am. Thanks."

The younger woman claps with delight when Mark places her Blue Aloha Mana Margarita before her. As he slides the whiskey sour toward the older woman, he checks for any kind of reaction—certainly nothing like the younger woman, of course, but perhaps a smile? But no. The woman isn't focused on him at all. In fact, she's not even looking at her drink. She's looking at the entrance. Now the younger woman stares at the entrance, too, and brings her hands to her mouth.

A tall man in his late twenties approaches their table, his gait unsteady and his posture unconfident, hands stuffed in his jacket pockets.

"Chad," the older woman exhales.

She stands and pushes back her chair and walks toward the man.

"Hey," she says softly. "You came. What the hell." She stops, looking unsure if she should embrace him or shake his hand or maybe put him up for adoption.

"Happy birthday, Mom," the man mumbles, his voice barely above a whisper, his gaze fixed on the floor, and then the older woman clutches onto him as if her life depended on it, a tear trickling down her face as he stands there awkwardly.

Meanwhile, the younger woman is bawling and sniffling and sucking her Blue Aloha Mana Margarita completely dry.

After the mother finally releases her son, the two take a seat, the man next to his mother and across from the younger woman.

"Welcome to Applebee's," Mark says sheepishly, handing the man a menu.

The older woman dabs at her eyes with a handkerchief. "I hope you're hungry," she tells her son. "There's a cake in the back big enough to feed the Ohio State football team."

"I'm starving," the son replies, and the older woman releases a fresh wail.

Mark returns to the bar, where Luna is observing the birthday table.

"Looks like it's a happy birthday after all," she says, then grabs a glass and pours a Coke and hands it to Mark. "Great work out there."

"I did nothing," Mark says, taking the glass, though he is surprised at how pleased he is to hear this from her.

Luna checks her watch. "I can't believe we have three more hours in our shift," she says.

I can stay here forever as long as I'm working with you, Mark wants to tell her.

"Yeah, time really stops here," he says instead.

They watch the mother and son and friend pointing at their menus, the two women talking and the man sitting quietly. Mark can't remember the last time he sat down for dinner with two other people. The younger woman says something that annoys the older woman again, and the older woman frowns, and yet their comfort with each other is abundantly clear to Mark, and it makes him feel wistful.

"Mark," Luna says, quietly.

Mark looks up. "Yes?"

She points at his section. "You better get back out there. Your other customers look hungry and neglected."

"Oh. Right." Mark dashes back to his section. On the way, he looks back at Luna, but she's facing the other way, reaching for a bottle on the top rack.

* * *

It's not that Mark dislikes living in Dayton. In fact, he very much feels at home in the Applebee's community he's found since moving back from Chicago. His colleagues and managers can be quirky, but they're the closest thing he has to a family. On some nights after his shift, he remains at work for a while, lounging about the bar with his colleagues and catching whatever event is on the television above the rows of bottles. The cost of living is reasonable. He enjoys the four seasons, the bright, cloudless days followed by dark, gloomy mornings. He's never felt unsafe—well, scratch that one. But sitting on his couch after work in the dark, when he considers giving Chicago a second chance—or *any* city, really, there's nothing holding him back—he honestly can't think of a single reason why he would leave, despite the current blanket of grief and mourning that covers the city. He knows his way around here. He knows it's up to him to put in the effort to make friends—his fellow servers at work have made it clear they want to hang out with him outside of work. He wishes—he just wishes—well, he's not exactly sure what he wishes, other than to have his mother back. He's never felt as lost as he does right now.

What he would do to get his hands on a manual for how to live magnificently.

Applebee's is a madhouse tonight, the first packed house since the shooting, and though Mark is already exhausted not even halfway through his shift, he's excited to see a big crowd. The customers are jovial and hungry, and they treat the harried servers with patience and kindness, exactly how Mark would expect for customers at a chain restaurant in the heart of the Midwest.

He swings by the bar, where Evan is mixing cocktails for a large party table. He likes Evan, but he wishes Luna were working tonight; she's faster and more precise, and the drink orders are beginning to stack up.

"Should I tell my section to ease up on their drinking?" Mark says.

Evan chuckles. "Nothing I can't handle," he says, which is not exactly true, but Mark throws him a shaka. Evan wipes his brow. "This is nutty. Tonight's tip-out should be amazing." Evan works three jobs while being a full-time student at the University of Dayton. Mark doesn't know how he manages it.

"Oh my! Is that Mark the server?" A familiar voice pipes up from behind him.

Mark is already grinning by the time he turns and sees Mabel Rogerson in a green floral dress and gray fedora making her way toward the bar.

"Queen Mabel," Mark breathes.

"Oh my, it *is* Mark! Hello, you hunk." Mabel embraces Mark before climbing onto a stool and laying her purse on the bar. She takes stock of her surroundings, then smacks her lips and prepares to get to business.

"Mabel," Mark says, grinning wider than he has in a while. "Did you come here just to see me?"

"Of course I did," Mabel exclaims. "But also, I was feeling parched." She smiles at Evan as he slides her a dish of peanuts. She squints at his name tag, then bats her eyelashes. "Hello, Evan, you handsome young man," she says. "This lady is dehydrated. Can I trouble you to make me a Blue Hawaiian Long Island Iced Tea?"

Mark bursts out laughing.

"Of course, ma'am," Evan says, reaching for a hurricane glass. "You just give me two clicks of this stopwatch."

Mabel winks at Mark, but his attention is on the restaurant entrance, where Luna is walking toward him, dressed in jeans and an Ohio State sweatshirt and Flyers cap.

"Oh, now who is *this*?" Mabel asks, peering back and forth between Mark and Luna. Her gaze settles on Mark. "Oh," she says, brightly. "*Ohhhhhh*."

"Luna, what are you doing here on your night off?" Mark asks.

For the first time that he can recall, Luna looks unsure of herself. "I was just in the area, um, and thought maybe I'd stop—" She looks at Mark to help her fill in the blank.

"What are you doing later tonight?" Mark asks.

Mabel, loudly crunching peanuts, swivels her head back and forth between the two.

"Oh, tonight?" Luna says. "I'm not sure, I haven't thought that far yet. How about you?"

"Ohhhh," Mabel says, quietly.

"Do you want to go roller skating with me?" Mark asks.

"Do I—roller skating?" Luna repeats.

Behind the bar, Evan subtly shakes his head. Mabel bites into a squeaky peanut, and Mark jumps.

"Um," Mark says, his face reddening. In the heat of the moment, the idea of roller skating sounded wonderful and appropriate, but now it sounds idiotic. He should have gone with bowling.

"I would love that," Luna says.

"You would?" Mark says.

"Ohhhh my," Mabel whispers.

In the next moment, which Mark will remember vividly decades later—along with the laughter from the boisterous crowds, the aroma of burgers frying in the kitchen, Evan in his periphery looking at him with pride and excitement—Luna smiles, a confident, haunting, glowing smile.

"I would," she says. She looks around. "I think I'll hang out here until then." She points at the bar stool by Mabel's. "Is this seat taken?" she asks Mabel.

"Not at all, sweetheart," Mabel says. "Oh my! What are you drinking, beautiful? I'm buying."

Evan clears his throat to get Mark's attention, then points at his section. "Sorry to be the one to say this," he says, "but your section looks like they're ready to riot." Evan looks again. "*Politely* riot," he adds.

"Ugh, right," Mark says. "You guys will hold down the fort here?"

"Oh, sweetie," Mabel says.

ACKNOWLEDGMENTS

I came to writing because of the books that once held me together. This book exists because of the people who helped me believe I could try. What follows is my attempt to thank them—the people who made this book, and the life behind it, possible.

I'm grateful to my parents and Kalena and Natalie, whose influences run through these pages.

I'm grateful to my friends, whose presence and encouragement carried me through the writing of this book, especially Cindy, Jamie, Char, Dan, Jorell, Adam, Gaye, Jerry, Leo, Jess, Jess, Susie, Balint, Scott, Ivan, Noel, Tomo, Cyndy, Jeff, and Amina.

I'm grateful to my communities at UNLV and the University of Houston, where I received the loving support that allowed these stories to take shape—at UNLV: Doug, Maile, Richard, Olivia, Vince, Julia, Xueyi, Kelly, Kaz, Lorinda, and Joe; and at the University of Houston: Pete, Alex, Toni, Boz, Chitra, Brenda, Jen, Hosam, Dave, Hunt, Tayyba, Pritha, and Maddie.

I'm grateful to Nicola and the team at Acre Books—Sarah, Sam, Barbara, and Ben—for their care, insight, and belief in this collection, and for bringing it into the world with such thoughtfulness.

Finally, I return with deepest gratitude to Pete, Alex, Doug, Hunt, Cindy, and Balint, who never stopped believing and who led me through the darkness when it all felt impossible.

The stories in this collection previously appeared in the following publications:
"Fortune of Forgetfulness," *Mississippi Review*
"Mother, Marksman," *The Georgia Review*
"Stay Brave, My Hercules," *McSweeney's Quarterly*
"Diesel Giovanni," *Mississippi Review*
"Surveillance [I and II]," *Chicago Quarterly Review*
"Sacrament of Confession," commissioned for *Selected Shorts* Comedy Project
"Paper Cranes," *The Southern Review*
"Gym Rut," *Prairie Schooner*
"Good Luck, Champ," *The Southern Review*